W9-CNL-798

DATE DUE			
SEP 2 0 '01			
OCT 2 4 '01			
NOV 1 6 '01			
JAN 1 7 '02			
FEB 1 5 '02			
FEB 2 8 '02			
43-14			
OCT 3 0 '03			
FEB 27 '06			
3-16-16			

Regarding the Fountain

A TALE, IN LETTERS, OF LIARS AND LEAKS

KATE KLISE

ILLUSTRATED BY M. SARAH KLISE

AN AVON CAMELOT BOOK

This is a work of fiction. Names, characters, places, and incidents either are the product of the author's imagination or are used fictitiously. Any resemblance to actual events, locales, organizations, or persons, living or dead, is entirely coincidental and beyond the intent of either the author or the publisher.

AVON BOOKS, INC.
1350 Avenue of the Americas
New York, New York 10019

Copyright © 1998 by Kate Klise
Interior illustrations copyright © 1998 by M. Sarah Klise
Layout and design by M. Sarah Klise with assistance from Matthew Willis
Published by arrangement with the author
Library of Congress Catalog Card Number: 97-18205
ISBN: 0-380-79347-4
www.avonbooks.com

First Avon Camelot Printing: April 1999
First Avon Books Hardcover Printing: April 1998

CAMELOT TRADEMARK REG. U.S. PAT. OFF. AND IN OTHER COUNTRIES, MARCA REGISTRADA, HECHO EN U.S.A.

Printed in the U.S.A.

OPM 10 9 8 7 6 5

This book is dedicated with love to our mother,
Marjorie A. Klise,
and the memory of our father,
Thomas S. Klise.

contents of this book were collected

The contents of this book were collected and organized by Sam N.'s fifth-grade class.

Dry Creek Middle School
Dry Creek, Missouri
"We Thirst for Knowledge"

September 1

Flowing Waters Fountains, Etc.
Watertown, CA

Dear Sir/Madam:

Would you please send a catalog of your products to our school? We need a new drinking fountain.

Please send the catalog to the attention of Mr. Walter Russ. He's the principal of our school.

Thank you very much.

Sincerely,

Goldie Fisch

Goldie Fisch
Secretary
Dry Creek Middle School

FLOWING WATERS FOUNTAINS, ETC.

September 8

Dry Creek Middle School
Dry Creek, MO

Hello, Goldie Fisch!

Thank you for writing to me. I love letters, don't you?

Regarding your request for a catalog of my fountains: I hope I won't disappoint you when I say that I don't have one. A catalog, I mean. I have plenty of fountains. I've built them all over the world. You may have seen some of my designs in hotels, palaces, parks and plazas.

I'd be delighted to build a drinking fountain for your school. But please understand that all of my fountains are custom-made. I'd have to visit your school and look around before I could design something for Dry Creek Middle School.

If this is okay with you, please drop me a note. (I don't have a phone. Hate the silly things.)

Again, thanks for writing.

Cheers,

Florence Waters

Florence Waters
President
Flowing Waters Fountains, Etc.

3

Dry Creek Middle School
Dry Creek, Missouri
"We Thirst for Knowledge"

Mr. Walter Russ
Principal

September 14

Flowing Waters Fountains, Etc.
Watertown, CA

Ms. Waters:

Perhaps you misunderstood the letter written earlier this month by the secretary of our school.

As per my request, Ms. Fisch wrote to you in the hopes of receiving information regarding a fountain. I am afraid, however, that she may not have made clear the nature of the fountain we are seeking.

While I'm sure the fountains you create for palaces and hotels are indeed lovely, we have no need for such extravagance in our school. Instead, what we are looking for is this:

Product:	drinking fountain
Style:	plain
Price:	modest

Would you please send the product description and price list of any fountains in your inventory that fit the above description?

Thank you for your time and cooperation.

Efficiently,

Mr. Walter Russ
Principal

WR/gf

4

eptember 27

ry Creek Middle School
ry Creek, MO

ear Mr. Wally Russ,

I received your letter ast week and, my good- ess, you sound just like ne author of the little ook of directions that ame with my blender.

I'm still not quite sure what your letter means (just s I'm not entirely certain how the blender works), but m guessing you'd like to see a catalog of my fountains. m I right? If so, I must repeat myself: I don't *have* a atalog of my fountains. I never build the same foun- ain twice.

But here's my idea: Why don't I come to your school ometime in the next week or two? I'll make a few rawings in my sketchbook. I'll return to my work- nop, begin construction, and bingo! Before you know , you'll have yourself a new fountain.

What do you say, Wally? *Florence Waters*

.S. By the by, in the future, try not to blame your con- ssion on other people. Goldie Fisch made the request r a catalog very clear the first time around.

M E M O

DATE: OCTOBER 1

TO: GOLDIE FISCH

FR: PRINCIPAL WALTER RUSS

RE: THE FOUNTAIN

Ms. Florence Waters will be visiting our school today.

As I will be in meetings all day, it will be your responsibility to show Ms. Waters where the leaky drinking fountain is located. It seems she needs to "see" the destination of her product before she can quote us a price on it.

You may need to impress upon her the fact that our desires regarding the fountain are purely functional. Dry Creek Middle School is neither a hotel nor a water park. Please remind Ms. Waters of this.

Also, in her letter, Ms. Waters addressed me as "Wally." Inform her that I prefer the unabbreviated version of "Walter."

FLOWING WATERS FOUNTAINS, ETC.

October 5

Dry Creek Middle School
Dry Creek, MO

Greetings, Goldie!

Thanks again for the wonderful tour of your school and town. What a charming little hamlet!

Oh yes, about the fountain. It should be fairly simple. Just a drinking fountain for the children, yes? That's easy enough. And it certainly won't take long to build.

There is one favor I would like to ask before I begin. A little teeny favor, actually.

Whenever I start a new fountain, I like to talk to the people who will see and use it once it's finished.

It's important to me to hear what they think the fountain should look like.

In this case, I'd like to hear from the students in the classroom located right next to the fountain. The sign on the door said MR. SAM N.'S FIFTH GRADERS. I knocked quietly, but no one answered the door. I guess they were out.

Goldie, would you do me the favor of giving my address to Mr. Sam N. and his students? Please ask them to send me their ideas for the fountain.

Thanks!

Your friend,

Flo Waters

P.S. I'm enclosing a sketch for you.

E __October 9__ HOUR __9:20__   (-2)

Sam N.

WHILE YOU WERE OUT

__Florence Waters, President__
__Flowing Waters Fountains, Etc.__
__Watertown, CA__

PHONE _____

□ Telephoned □ Returned Call □ Left Package
□ Please Call ☒ Was In □ Please See Me
□ Will Call Again ☒ Won't Call □ Important

MESSAGE: __Florence Waters, the fountain__
__designer, stopped by your classroom__
__to speak to your students last__
__week when you were all out on a__
__field trip. No need to call her__
__back (she doesn't have a phone), but__
__she would like to hear your stu-__
__dents' ideas regarding the fountain.__
                                    __Goldie J.__

Signed ___Goldie J.___

FIFTH-GRADE ANNOUNCEMENTS

October 10th

TODAY'S WRITING ASSIGNMENT:

As you all know, our school needs a new drinking fountain. A fountain designer by the name of Florence Waters has been asked to design one for us. Before she does, Ms. Waters would like to hear what you think the new fountain should look like. Write a short paragraph or two describing your ideas for the perfect drinking fountain.

Because Ms. Waters prefers to communicate* by letter, we will mail our ideas to her tomorrow.

Mr. N.

HISTORY CLUB MEETING: 3:30 TODAY

*WORD OF THE DAY: communicate. To interchange thoughts, feelings, or ideas.

HOMEWORK

GET READY
CARVING
CONTEST
(need more
pumpkins!)

VERMEER

October 10

Dear Florence Waters,

Hello. My name is Tad Poll.

I'm very glad we're getting a new drinking fountain. The old one is awful!! It leaks all the time, so there's always a huge puddle around it. Bleh!!!

As long as you're building a new fountain, I think you should make it different (and better) than the old boring (and leaky) kind. Can you make it so that the water comes out in a loop-the-loop? I'll draw a picture to show you what I mean.

      Sincerely,

         Tad

10/10

Hi, Ms. Waters!

We wish the new fountain could be big enough so that we could splash around in it **between classes.**

Love,

     Lily **and Paddy**

10 October

Dear Ms. Waters,

I am in 5th grade. I am writing to you about the fountain.

Once when I was on vacation, I saw a glass-bottomed boat. It was like a regular boat, only it had glass in the bottom so you could look down and see all the fish in the water.

Do you think maybe you could do this with the fountain at our school? Instead of glass-bottomed, make it a glass-sided fountain. That way, we could put fish in our fountain. It would be like an aquarium and a drinking fountain all in one.

I like fish. Last year I did a report on tropical fish for science fair. Goldie Fisch let me use her aquarium.

Yours truly,
Minnie O.

October 10

Dear Fountain Designer,

When you build the fountain for our school, do you think it would be possible to have other things come out of it besides just water? Maybe there could be different buttons for things like lemonade, chocolate milk, and root beer. (Maybe even chocolate shakes????)

Yours truly,

Shelly and Gil

P.S.   Fifth graders rule!!

Dry Creek Middle School
Dry Creek, MO

October 10

Ms. Florence Waters
President
Flowing Waters Fountains, Etc.

Dear Ms. Waters,

My students have enjoyed using their imaginations to design the perfect drinking fountain.
I like Lily and Paddy's idea of making the drinking fountain big enough to splash around in between classes. While you're at it, maybe you can
add a hot tub and whirlpool for the teachers to
splash around in after school.

Hey, a teacher can dream, can't he?

With kind regards,

Sam N.

Mr. Sam N.
Fifth-grade teacher

P.S. Sorry we missed you when you came to visit
our school. My class was on a field trip to the Dry
Creek County Courthouse. We're working on a
research project about our town's history.

October 15th

Dearest Fifth-Grade Class:

What lovely letters you write! And what wonderful artists you are! Your drawings are hanging in my studio. Pure inspiration. Of course a drinking fountain should have tropical fish and chocolate shakes! Brilliant.

Keep the ideas flowing.

Yours in fountains, *Florena*

P.S. The school seemed so quiet when I was there. Is it always? I'm in the process of cleaning out my attic. Well, not cleaning really. Just rearranging. Anyway, I came across some old musical instruments I think you might like. The sound of the harp is quite breathtaking. The French horns are nice, too. The guitars are from a mariachi band I once played with. If it's okay, I'll have the instruments delivered later this week to Dry Creek Middle School, c/o Mr. Sam N.'s fifth-grade class. Think of it as compensation for sending me your wonderful ideas for the fountain.

P.P.S. Is there really a creek in Dry Creek? Is it really dry?

16

October 20

TO:
Florence Waters
President
Flowing Waters Fountains, Etc.

This is a letter from the fifth graders who wanted to

Holler "THANKS" for sending us those cool instruments

And tell you we're forming a fifth-grade band that will make musical

Noises which Mr. N. says will drive him

Krazy and give him tension headaches

So if you find any earplugs in your attic you may want to send them to him! Thanks again!

Tad on violin.

Minnie on harp

Gil on French horn

Lily on guitar

Shelly on trombone

Paddy on drums and cymbal

P.S. Yes, we do have a creek here. And yes, it is dry. We're researching the history of Dry Creek for a class project. So far we've learned that our town used to be called Spring Creek. That was a long time ago, before the spring dried up which caused the creek to dry up, too. We'll keep you posted as we learn more.

17

PRESS RELEASE

For Immediate Release   Contact: Goldie Fisch
October 30   Dry Creek Middle School

SCHOOL BOARD CONSIDERS NEW FOUNTAIN;
FIFTH GRADE "BANDS" TOGETHER

Dry Creek, MO — The Dry Creek School Board voted today to conduct a feasibility study regarding the installation of a new drinking fountain. The only dissenting vote was that of School Board President Sally Mander.

Ms. Mander believes the present fountain can and should be fixed. She offered to contact Delbert "Dee" Eel at Dry Creek Water Company.

"Dee Eel is an expert in these things," Mander said. "He installed the drinking fountain when the school was built. I'm sure he'll be able to fix it."

The meeting adjourned with Mander's words: "It's too darn hot to worry about this. Let's all go swimming at my pool!" In addition to serving as school board president, Mander also owns Dry Creek Swimming Pool.

On a lighter note, the fifth-grade class of Mr. Sam N. has formed a musical band. The students plan to call the group Sam N.'s Tune-A-Combo.

SALLY MANDER

DELBERT EEL

DRY CREEK SWIMMING POOL

CRYSTAL-CLEAR ALL YEAR   TEMPERATURE-CONTROLLED   YEAR-ROUND FUN

···

FAX

October 30
11:37 P.M.

FOR YOUR EYES ONLY

    TO: Dee Eel
             President
             Dry Creek Water Co.

    FR: Sally Mander
             Chief Executive Officer
             Dry Creek Swimming Pool

    RE: The fountain

CONFIDENTIAL

Dee:

You fool! And to think I trusted you!

You said you'd taken care of that "leak." NOW look where we are. If they install a new fountain, it's over — for you and me both!

What have you got to say for yourself?

Sally

P.S. Respond by mail or fax. I don't want you calling me here at the swimming pool anymore. I'm afraid my phone might be tapped.

END OF TRANSMISSION

···

A JEWEL OF A POOL

DRY CREEK WATER COMPANY

"Where Clean Water Is A 'D-EEL!'"
Bringing You the Very Best Water for 29 Years

Delbert "Dee" Eel
President

October 31

PRIVATE

Dearest Sally,

Let's not lose our heads.

Granted, the decision by the school board to consider replacing my (okay, "our") fountain is unfortunate. (And I won't remind you that you said you had the members of the school board wrapped around your finger.)

But not to worry. They've only agreed to *study* the matter. These things take time. They'll never find enough money in the budget to actually *buy* a new drinking fountain.

Strategy: You stall. You *are* still an expert in *that*, I trust. (And by the way, nice move inviting everyone over for a swim last night.) I'll see what I can do about the "leak." Together, we'll keep a lid on it — so to speak.

Dee

Dry Creek Middle School
Dry Creek, Missouri
"We Thirst for Knowledge"

November 3

Flowing Waters Fountains, Etc.
Watertown, CA

Hi, Florence!

Thank you so much for sending the drawing of me. I have it on my desk and have received lots of compliments on it. What a nice friend you are! I hope you'll let me treat you to lunch next time you're in town. I promise I won't take you to our school cafeteria. Today's menu was baloney pizza and pigs-in-a-blanket.

That reminds me, Principal Russ asked me to tell you that he's waiting for your bid on the fountain. He needs to know how much it's going to cost. ("To the penny," he says.) From what I understand, a battle is underway between Mr. Walter Russ and Ms. Sally Mander. She's the president of the school board. She also owns the local swimming pool and is probably the richest person in Dry Creek after Delbert "Dee" Eel, of course. He owns the local water company.

Anyway, I hope I'll see you again. In the meantime, I look forward to seeing your ideas for the new drinking fountain.

Your friend,

Goldie Fisch

Secretary
Dry Creek Middle School

November 10

Dry Creek Middle School
Dry Creek, MO

Hi, Goldie!

Thanks for the note. It's always a treat to hear from friends. But really, Goldie, I'm concerned about your diet. Baloney pizza? Pigs-in-a-blanket? Hogwash! I'm sending you a picnic basket filled with goodies to supplement the cafeteria fare. Try the clover honey on the pumpkin muffins. My bees did such a lovely job this year.

Speaking of working like a bee: Given your busy workload, why does your boss make you write all his letters for him? He is the principal, isn't he? You'd think he'd be able to write his own letters.

Tell him I'll be happy to answer any questions he has regarding the fountain, so long as he writes to me himself. (Unless of course both of his hands are broken, in which case please tell him how terribly sorry I am.)

Now, Goldie, just between you and me, the sketches for the fountain are coming along quite nicely, if I do say so myself. I'll enclose a few ideas I'm kicking around. The suggestions from the students were enormously helpful.

Take care, Goldie!

Flo

November 13

Flowing Waters Fountains, Etc.
Watertown, CA

Dear Florence,

Mr. N. is letting us stay in from recess to study for our spelling test, but we'd rather write you a letter.

That was Lily. Now this is Paddy. We're taking turns writing paragraphs. Hmmmm, let's see. What can I write? Nothing is new in Dry Creek. Nothing's ever new here. This is the world's most B-O-R-I-N-G town.

My turn. (This is Lily.) Paddy's right. Dry Creek IS a boring town and Dry Creek Middle School is the world's most **BORING** school. At least we're lucky we got a good teacher this year. Mr. N. is pretty OK.

Paddy here. I just thought of something to tell you, Florence. Your name was in the newspaper last week. We'll send you the article.

This is Lily again. We better sign off because Mr. N. is walking this wa——

This is Sam. And if this note were addressed to anyone other than you, Ms. Waters, it would be in the garbage. But being the "pretty OK" teacher that I am, I'll stick this letter and the newspaper clipping in an envelope and mail it myself. (Here it is first semester and already I'm breaking my own rules. I'm doomed.)

ld Drinking Fountain "All Wet," Says Principal

RINKING FOUNTAIN

In a nearly unanimous decision, the Dry Creek School Board voted to begin a study regarding the installation of a new drinking fountain in the fifth-grade hallway.

Ms. Florence Waters of Flowing Waters untains, Etc. has been asked to submit a bid d design for the project.

Opposed to the study is Sally Mander, pres-ent of the school board and owner of Dry eek Swimming Pool.

"The current drinking fountain is just fine," said Mander. "Okay, so it leaks a little bit. Big deal. We can fix it. But noooo! We've got to buy a new fountain! What kind of lesson does this send to our children? When something breaks, do we just get rid of it? This

SALLY MANDER

one more example of how we've become a owaway society. It's a sad day for the town Dry Creek."

(Continued on page 2, column 1)

CECE SALT

CeCe Salt Pulling Hair Out Over Bad Perm

Anyone who has seen Cecelia "CeCe" Salt around town lately knows she's not happy.

"I am never going back to the Curl and Twirl," CeCe Salt announced to the lunch crowd gathered at the Dry Creek Cafe. "This is the worst permanent I have ever had."

Pearl O. Ster, owner of Pearl's Curl and Twirl, explained what happened.

"I couldn't rinse the perm solution out fast enough," said Ster, a native of Dry Creek. "By the time I got all the bottles of water open and poured on her head, it was too late. People don't realize how hard it is to give a perm

(Continued on page 2, column 2)

PRINCIPAL RUSS

(From page 1)
In response, Principal Walter Russ said: "According to school records, the drinking fountain has leaked ever since the school was built. Requests to have it repaired have been ignored repeatedly by Delbert 'Dee' Eel.

"Frankly, I'm tired of the blasted thing," Russ continued. "The leak at the base of the fountain is both unsightly and dangerous. Only last week, I myself slipped in the puddle. I spent the rest of the day with soggy pants and smelling like a wet dog. I wonder if Ms. Mander would enjoy working under such conditions."

Ms. Mander responded by suggesting that Principal Russ consider wearing a diaper. "He's always been a big baby, anyway," said Mander.

(From page 1)
when you're using bottled water."

Ster offered Salt a free permanent, but the longtime customer refused.

"Next time I'm going to the salon in Springfield," said CeCe Salt, clearly shaken by the ordeal.

FLOWING WATERS FOUNTAINS, ETC.

November 18

Dear Lily and Paddy,

I adored your note written duet-style. But honestly, I can't believe your town and school are as B O R I N G as you say. Surely there are exciting things to do and see in Dry Creek.

For example – and keep this under your hat – I would pay money to see a principal shuffling around school with soggy pants and smelling like a wet dog. I hope the poor man wasn't badly hurt, was he? Did you see him fall? What a sight that must have been!

I'll send you some of my old camera equipment. If it happens again, snap a picture for me, would you? Or sketch the scene for me. I cherish your drawings.

Take care, dears!

Yours in adventures,

Florence

P.S. Please tell your teacher to call me Florence. And tell him I've made a career out of breaking rules.

FIFTH-GRADE ANNOUNCEMENTS

November 21

SPELLING TEST: Tomorrow

HISTORY CLUB MEETING: 3:30 TODAY

ART: Everybody ready for a new bulletin board? I'll dig out the art supplies. You decide on a theme.*

Mr. N.

*WORD OF THE DAY: theme. 1. A principal subject or idea embodied in a work of art. 2. A topic for discussion, often expressed in a phrase or question.

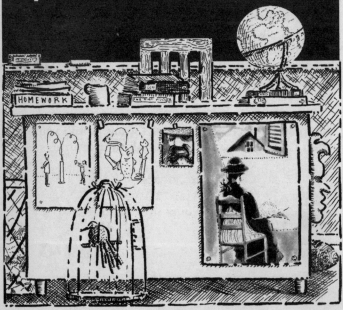

28

DRY CREEK MIDDLE SCHOOL

<u>M E M O</u>

DATE: NOVEMBER 23

TO: GOLDIE FISCH

FR: PRINCIPAL WALTER RUSS

RE: THE FOUNTAIN

Where is the proposal and bid from Florence Waters? I requested it weeks ago. Please place it front and center on my desk.

Mr. Russ,
As I mentioned to you some time ago, Florence has asked that you write to her yourself for information regarding the fountain. She feels that as principal, you should be able to write your own letters.

Respectfully,

Goldie Fisch

November 24

Regarding: The Fountain

Ms. Waters:

I must receive a proposal from you for the replacement drinking fountain as soon as possible. We need to see an official bid and design study before we can approve funding for the project.

As you may know, this is a matter of some friction between School Board President Sally Mander and myself. She thinks the old fountain can be fixed; I know we need a new one.

Meanwhile, the leak at the base of the fountain continues to worsen. I don't care if the children enjoy sloshing through the puddle. It's dangerous. (I should know. I slipped again this morning.)

Also, I'm sure I need not remind you that we are requesting a bid for a simple, no-frills, upright standard drinking fountain. In passing Mr. Sam N.'s classroom yesterday, I noticed a bulletin board display entitled "Fountain Fantasies" onto which were attached assorted fanciful depictions of outlandish fountains.

I further understand that the children have sent you similar drawings. At the risk of stating the obvious, I will tell you that Mr. Sam N. is one of our more "creative" teachers.

He makes it a practice to assign his students highly "creative" projects of little or no practical purpose. Needless to say, none of the designs seen on the bulletin board or submitted by the children need be incorporated into your proposal.

Again, please send your bid to my attention as soon as possible, or sooner.

Authoritatively,

Walter Russ

Mr. Walter Russ

P.S. I will appreciate it if, in the future, you will refrain from involving yourself in the business of my administrative procedures. I will run this office the way I see fit. I'm the boss around here. If I don't like writing letters (and I don't), I shouldn't have to. That's Goldie Fisch's job. (Or it was anyway.)

Thanks for the cameras, Florence!

Lily and Paddy

FLOWING WATERS FOUNTAINS, ETC.

November 30

Wally Russ
Principal
Dry Creek Middle School
Dry Creek, MO

My dear man,

Forgive me for saying so, but shame on you.

I'm beginning to believe that you're one of those worrisome bean counters who see everything (letters, fountains, life . . .) and everyone (students, secretaries, teachers, artists . . .) in terms of numbers and procedures and plans and, well, I'm afraid I simply can't work that way.

Don't you realize the children in your school are thirsting for more than just water to cool their dry throats? They thirst for beauty, art, joy, adventure. And you want to know how much it will cost? You can't put a timetable or a price tag on these things. Some things in life cannot be rushed. The fountain is one of them. Please let's not discuss such matters again.

Wally, I must say that you strike me as an extremely tense man. Have you ever considered aqua-therapy? Maybe some aerobic sloshing through the puddle three or four times per week could do you some good. Or perhaps water ballet? I used to direct a water ballet company in Fiji. I'll enclose a guide to some of the more basic moves. Practice these daily and I promise you'll become a more graceful and composed gentleman.

Aesthetically yours,

Florence Waters

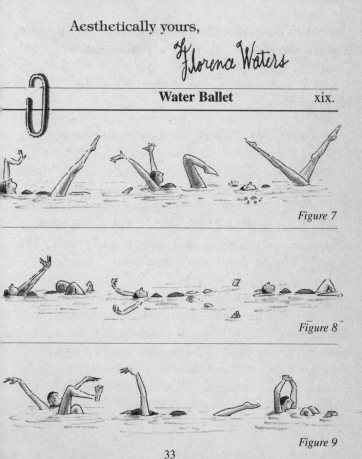

Water Ballet xix.

Figure 7

Figure 8

Figure 9

Dry Creek Middle School
Dry Creek, MO

December 5

Ms. Florence Waters
Flowing Waters Fountains, Etc.

Hi, Florence.

How are you? I'm fine — except BUSY. Our class is working on the town history project. If we finish in time, Mr. N. wants us to read our "History of Dry Creek" during Dry Creek Days in May.

Our band is going to perform a few songs for the ceremony. Mr. N. says we're starting to sound pretty good. He took the earplugs out, so I guess that's a good sign.

Well, I better go. Hope you're doing OK, and that you haven't forgotten about us or the fountain.

Yours truly,

Gil

il
o Dry Creek Middle School
ifth-Grade Class
ry Creek, MO
.S.A.

ear Gil:

Of course I haven't forgotten about you or the drinking
untain!

In fact, I've thought of little else since I arrived in Spain
vo weeks ago. Had a craving for *tapas* (Spanish snacks) and
audí (my favorite architect). I'm also collecting design
eas for the fountain.

What's this I hear about a bulletin board in your room
led with more ideas for the fountain? I'd love to see them.
ill you please send the drawings to me at my home
ldress? I have my mail forwarded when I travel.

Gracias, amigo!

Adios,   Florence

S. I picked up a trunkful of costumes at the flea market
re. Am sending along for you and the class. Band uni-
ms, perhaps?

FIFTH-GRADE ANNOUNCEMENTS

December 20th

ASSIGNMENTS:

Math: Page 117, ALL

History of Dry Creek: Let's start putting together a timeline for Dry Creek. We can add new information as we go.

Also, another package has arrived from the ever-intriguing* Florence Waters. Should we open before lunch or after lunch?

Vote Here

Open before lunch   Open after lunch

✓ ✓ ✓ ✓ ✓ ✓

*WORD OF THE DAY: intrigue. 1. To spark the interest or curiosity of. 2. A covert scheme to achieve a secret purpose; an underhand plot.

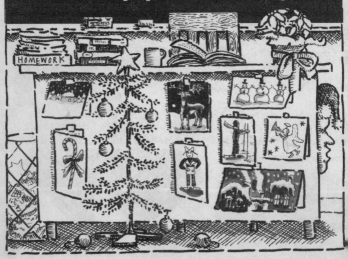

36

DRY CREEK SWIMMING POOL

STAL-CLEAR ALL YEAR   TEMPERATURE-CONTROLLED   YEAR-ROUND FUN

....

FAX

ecember 29
:15 P.M.

CONFIDENTIAL

TO: Dee Eel
           President
           Dry Creek Water Co.

FR: Sally Mander
           Chief Executive Officer
           Dry Creek Swimming Pool

RE: The fountain

ee:

ell???? Is the "leak" fixed or not?

n glad you have such a casual attitude about what
ould very well be the end of both our careers.

ill you please let me know what's going on?

END OF TRANSMISSION

....

A JEWEL OF A POOL

DRY CREEK WATER COMPANY

"Where Clean Water Is A 'D-EEL!'"
Bringing You the Very Best Water for 30 Years

Delbert "Dee" Eel
President

January 2

Sally,

I do take this whole drinking fountain business very seriously. If they find out about the you-know-what under the you-know-what … Well, YOU know what could happen.

Don't worry. We're not in hot water (ha ha) yet.

PRIVATE

Dry Creek Middle School
Dry Creek, MO

January 5

Ms. Florence Waters
Flowing Waters Fountains, Etc.

Dear Florence,

Thank you very, very, very much for sending us the clothes from Spain! They're perfect uniforms for our band. We look (and even sound!) a million times better when we wear the costumes. We'll send pictures so you can see for yourself how GREAT we look.

The Fifth-Grade Band (a.k.a. Sam N.'s Tune-A-Combo)

P.S. We're also enclosing our latest ideas for the drinking fountain.

menu
straws
cups
microwave
candy
chips
forks
spoons

☐ water
☐ hot chocolate
☐ strawberry shake
☐ lemon ice
☐ push for more options

Dry Creek Middle School
Dry Creek, MO

January 9

Dear Florence,

My students are still talking about you. They were delighted with the gifts you sent them from Spain — you are too generous — and even more by your sincere interest in their ideas for the fountain.

The class has been discussing the best way to thank you for all the great things you've sent us this year. Our idea? We want you to be our guest at Dry Creek Days.

Now, I'm sure it can't compare to the festivals you've attended in Europe. But given the size of our little town, we really do put on a nice show during Dry Creek Days.

Every year during the last weekend in May, the citizens of Dry Creek do nothing but eat, dance, sing, and risk life and limb on the carnival rides. For an entire weekend, we live on corn dogs, homemade pie, and cotton candy. (In fact, we eat so much cotton candy during Dry Creek Days, no one can even look at the stuff the rest of the year.)

This year's celebration should be extra special because it marks the anniversary of two important events in our town's history. Thirty years ago this year, Dry Creek Middle School was built. It's also the 30th anniversary of the year the creek dried up. In studying the history of Dry Creek, my class is learning what a pivotal event this was. I'll have them send you their work-in-progress: "The History of Dry Creek." The students are researching and writing the whole thing themselves.

Anyway, we'd love to have you as our guest at Dry Creek Days. Hope you'll consider our offer to come visit in May.

Crossing my fingers,

Sam N.

Enclosure: "The History of Dry Creek" (first draft)

(After reading the enclosed, maybe you can understand why we all feel the need to gorge ourselves on cotton candy and corn dogs one weekend out of every year. It helps us forget the beautiful future we have behind us.)

THE HISTORY OF DRY CREEK
by the Fifth-Grade Class

Years ago when the spring still flowed, residents of Dry Creek (then called Spring Creek) filled their jugs and pitchers with fresh water from the spring. Kids swam and played in the creek. With the unlimited supply of clean water, farmers were able to grow just about anything they wanted.

All that changed 30 years ago. Now we have to buy all our water from Delbert ("Dee") Eel at the Dry Creek Water Company. Farmers can't afford to grow anything because the cost of irrigation is so high. Most people and businesses have moved away.

Florence: That's as far as we've gotten. We've had to do all the research ourselves because the town historian, Liz Ard (she's Sally Mander's sister), lost most of the documents dating back to the days when Dry Creek was still Spring Creek.

We're interviewing people who have lived here a long time and still remember the good old days. We hope to finish in time for Dry Creek Days. And we REALLY hope you'll come visit during Dry Creek Days so you can hear our town history report AND see our first concert performance.

Please say YES!!!

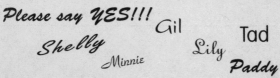

Gil

Shelly

Minnie

Lily

Tad

Paddy

43

TELL-A-GRAM
The Old-Timey Telegram Company

Sent from: F. Waters
Lusaka, Zambia AFRICA

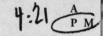

Sent to: Fifth-Grade Class
Dry Creek Middle School
Dry Creek, MO USA

YES - STOP - INVITATION TO DRY CREEK DAYS

ACCEPTED - STOP - IN AFRICA COLLECTING

TROPICAL PLANTS FOR FOUNTAIN - STOP - AM

SENDING PAIR OF LION-HEADED MARMOSETS

(MONKEYS) FOR CLASS - STOP - HOPE THIS

ISN'T PROBLEM - STOP - HOW CURIOUS THAT

SCHOOL BUILT AND CREEK DRIED UP IN SAME

YEAR - STOP -

-FLO

PS - FOUND TROPICAL WATER LILY (BLUE

GIGANTEA) WITH STALK SO LARGE, CAN BE

USED AS SNORKEL - STOP - DO YOU ALL HAVE

WET SUITS - STOP JAN 1 8 PM

Form 1801

44

January 26

Florence Waters
Flowing Waters Fountains, Etc.

Hi, Florence.

Hooray!!! We're so happy you're coming in May!

We're writing a song for the band to play at Dry Creek Days. Here are the lyrics:

Our town is dull
In fact, it's a bore
So we won't be offended
If you start to snore

But our assignment this year
Is a historical story
About our hometown
And its lack of glory

So make yourselves comfortable
Kick off your shoes
And get ready to hear
A history in blues.

That's all we've got so far. Writing songs is harder than we thought. But now that we know you're coming, we're determined to make it especially good!

Well, we gotta go to band practice. See ya!
Tad *and Shelly*
P.S. We love the monkeys! Thanks a million!

ATHENS, GREECE

February 4

Dear Tad and Shelly,

What a marvelous idea! I absolutely ADORE original music. (I was once engaged to a Russian composer, but goodness, that's another story.)

Anyway, I simply can't wait until May to hear your work, so I'm sending a parcel of recording equipment (tape recorders, microphones, etcetera). Would you mind recording your song for me and sending it to my home address? I'll return there after I gather a few more thingumadoodles for the fountain.

Love to all – or "agape" as they say here. (It's pronounced like this: Ahhh-gaaahh-pay.) It means giving love without expecting anything back. Lovely idea, isn't it?

Speaking of which, perhaps you'd like to share the tape recorders with your classmates.

Florence

FIFTH-GRADE ANNOUNCEMENTS

February 6th

ASSIGNMENTS:
- **Science:** Lab reports due next Monday
- **Spelling Test:** Friday

REMEMBER: On Friday we need to wrap up our interviews for "The History of Dry Creek." Be ready to hit the streets with notebooks and questions to ask longtime residents about their memories of our town. Don't forget to ask for interesting anecdotes* about the early days of Dry Creek, back when it was called Spring Creek. If you turn up any new information, please post it on our timeline.

Thanks, Tad and Shelly, for donating the box of tape recorders to the supply closet! These will be great for recording interviews. If you want to check out a tape recorder, write your name on the sign-out sheet.

Mr. N.

*WORD OF THE DAY: anecdote. 1. A short retelling of an interesting or funny incident. 2. The secret or hitherto unpublished particulars of history or biography.

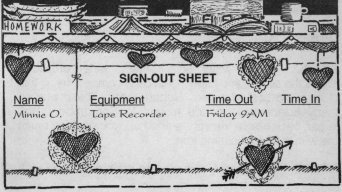

SIGN-OUT SHEET

Name	Equipment	Time Out	Time In
Minnie O.	Tape Recorder	Friday 9AM	

INTERVIEW TRANSCRIPT

Interview Subject: Pearl O. Ster
Reporter: Minnie O.
Interview location: Pearl's Curl and Twirl
Interview date: February 7

MINNIE: Pearl, you've lived in Dry Creek all your life. What do you remember about the old days?

PEARL: You mean way back when, when it was still Spring Creek? Now, honey, don't get me started 'cause I'll cry like a baby.

MINNIE: Why?

PEARL: Why? Well, don't you know back in the old days I was the best beautician in the entire state? I won awards for my ducktails and chignons. People came to the Curl and Twirl by the busload for my special spring water shampoo and scalp treatments. Now look at this shop — empty. And look at my appointment book — blank.

MINNIE: What happened?

PEARL: Everybody started going to the salons in Springfield.

MINNIE: How come?

PEARL: Better water and stronger water pressure. That's the secret, you know. I just can't compete using this clumsy old bottled water. Nobody can. That's why so many businesses up and moved to Springfield. But, sugar, back before the spring dried up, you couldn't touch me with a 20-foot curling iron.

MINNIE: Do you remember when the spring dried up?

2.

PEARL: Remember it? Honey, I still have nightmares about it. It was the day the new middle school opened. I know because I was putting color on Cora Reef's hair. You probably don't remember Cora, but she was the science teacher. She wanted to look real nice for the unveiling ceremonies of the new school.

MINNIE: What happened?

PEARL: You don't want to know.

MINNIE: Please?

PEARL: Well, Cora got color, all right. Hot pink. Makes me dizzy just thinking about it. I was using my special Red Hairing Formula. My own secret recipe, of course. I used it all the time on Cora to bring out her natural red highlights. I always left it on for 12 minutes exactly. No more. No less. Timing is critical in this business. So as soon as the timer buzzed at 12 minutes, I put Cora under the water faucet and turned it on. Nothing. No water. The spring had gone and dried up on me. By the time I bought some bottled water from Dee Eel, it was too late. The Red Hairing Formula had been on Cora's head for over an hour. Poor thing looked like a wild flamingo that'd been struck by lightning. Hurt my teeth just to look at her. And, honey, was she mad! First dissatisfied customer I ever had.

(Sound of sniffles)

MINNIE: Don't cry, Pearl.

PEARL: I'm sorry. I just can't help myself sometimes. You better run along.

MINNIE: Well, thanks for helping with our history project.

PEARL: Oh, don't mention it. Here, let me French-braid your hair before you go. At least I don't need water for that.

HISTORY OF DRY CREEK

100 Years Ago

Spring Creek settled

75 Years Ago

MELON

Population tripl

Spring Creek farmers harvest recur yields of rice, melon and cucumbers

Spring Creek becomes fish farming capital of U.S.

Vacationers come to Spring Creek to see exotic flora and fauna

DRY CREEK SWIMMING POOL

FAX

February 7
2:53 P.M.

CONFIDENTIAL

TO: Dee Eel
President
Dry Creek Water Co.

FR: Sally Mander
Chief Executive Officer
Dry Creek Swimming Pool

RE: The fountain

READ AND DESTROY

Dee:

I'm sorry I called you a drip the other day, but this whole fountain thing makes me nervous. And how many times do I have to tell you not to talk about the you-know-what in public? You never know who might be listening.

Would you please keep me updated on where we are? Regarding the fountain, I mean.

Sally

END OF TRANSMISSION

A JEWEL OF A POOL

DRY CREEK WATER COMPANY

"Where Clean Water Is A 'D-EEL!'"
Bringing You the Very Best Water for 30 Years

Delbert "Dee" Eel
President

ebruary 8   PRIVATE

al:

pologies for "drip" remark accepted.

was over at the school yesterday, trying to patch things
p with Walter Russ. He insists the "leak" underneath
he fountain can't be fixed. And of course he's right.

till, I'm trying to convince him that all he needs is a super-
uper sponge mat installed on the floor near the fountain
— as I put it — "absorb the excess sweat produced by
he condensation of the fountain." My new strategy:
onfuse him until we can think of something better.

don't know what's going on, but it seems like the "leak"
getting worse (i.e. stronger) all the time. I'll try to get
ver there every morning before school starts so I can
op up around the fountain base.

here is one good thing to report: From what I've heard,
lowing Waters Fountains, Etc. still hasn't submitted a
roposal for a new fountain to the principal. Do you
now anything about this Florence Waters character?
et's try to dig up some dirt on her.

lso, see what you can do to stall Principal Russ. You
now, give him the old run-around. You were always
ood at that, Sal.

53

SALLY MANDER
CHIEF EXECUTIVE OFFICER
DRY CREEK SWIMMING POOL

February 9

Mr. Walter Russ
Principal
Dry Creek Middle School

Dear Mr. Russ:

This petty squabble we seem to be having over a small, insignificant fountain really is silly of us, isn't it? Especially now with Dry Creek Days quickly approaching. Speaking of which, I have an idea that I think will delight both you and the charming students at your lovely school.

Instead of squandering our precious resources on something foolish like books, desks, or a new drinking fountain, why don't we buy something the children will *really* like? Are you thinking what I'm thinking? That's right: Ice Cream.

We've never had ice cream at Dry Creek Days before. Wouldn't this be a nice treat for children of all ages? Instead of spending the money on a new drinking fountain, I vote for ice cream. In fact, I Scream for Ice Cream!

And talk about quenching your thirst. There's nothing like a cold ice cream cone to do the trick.

In fact, it would be my pleasure to buy you an ice cream cone sometime. Or even a sundae. Do you like banana splits? I know I do.

Mr. Russ — may I call you Walter? — we don't see nearly enough of one another during the school year. And when we do, it's a shame to spend it arguing over small, silly things like leaky drinking fountains.

School will be out in a few short months. Surely the leak (really, it's more like a little puddle) around the base of the drinking fountain will dry up during the heat of summer.

Let's you and me toast our new friendship with a tasty ice cream cone AND some delicious conversation. Drop me a line and we'll arrange a time and place.

Your friend and admirer,

Sally Mander

P.S. Do you like to go swimming, Walter? Who doesn't, right? I'm enclosing a summer pass to my swimming pool. Look forward to seeing you!

SALLY MANDER'S
DRY CREEK SWIMMING POOL

Swimmer's Name: *Walter Russ*
Good For: *Summer swim*

A JEWEL OF A POOL

M E M O

DATE: FEBRUARY 11

TO: GOLDIE FISCH

FR: PRINCIPAL WALTER RUSS

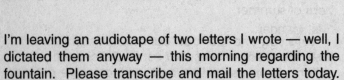

RE: THE FOUNTAIN

I'm leaving an audiotape of two letters I wrote — well, I dictated them anyway — this morning regarding the fountain. Please transcribe and mail the letters today. You may need to work through lunch.

Dry Creek Middle School
Dry Creek, Missouri
"We Thirst for Knowledge"

Mr. Walter Russ
Principal

February 11

Ms. Sally Mander
President, Dry Creek School Board
c/o Dry Creek Swimming Pool

Ms. Mander:

I do not think it would be wise for us to meet for ice cream — be it cone, sundae, or banana split. And no, I do not think the students of Dry Creek Middle School would be better served by ice cream instead of a new drinking fountain.

The condition of the fountain worsens daily. (I slipped in the puddle *again* this morning and nearly broke a lower vertebra.)

I am proceeding with plans to install a new drinking fountain — just as soon as I receive the bid and design plan from Flowing Waters Fountains, Etc.

Firmly,

Mr. Walter Russ
Principal

WR/gf

Dry Creek Middle School
Dry Creek, Missouri
"We Thirst for Knowledge"

Mr. Walter Russ
Principal

February 11

Ms. Florence Waters
President
Flowing Waters Fountains, Etc.

Ms. Waters:

We still have not received information from you regarding either the design or the cost estimate of the proposed drinking fountain.

I understand from your letter (11/30) that you are not accustomed to working under the restrictions of budgets or deadlines. Let me remind you that we are a publicly funded school. As such, we are accountable to the taxpayers of Dry Creek.

The Dry Creek School Board will vote soon on the purchase of a new fountain. We'll need to see your plans for the fountain before then.

Sternly,

Walter Russ

Mr. Walter Russ
Principal

WR/gf

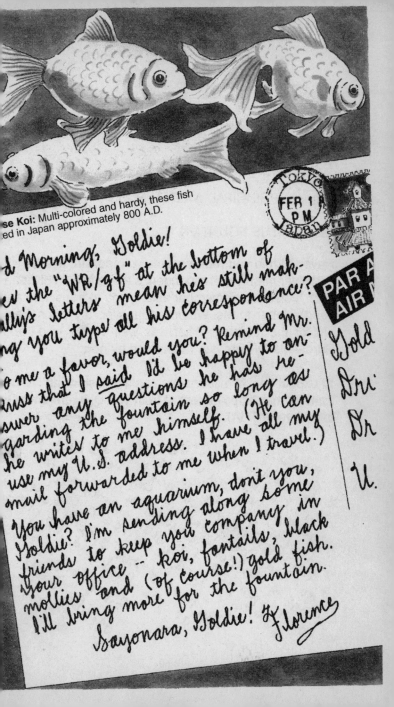

se Koi: Multi-colored and hardy, these fish
ed in Japan approximately 800 A.D.

TOKYO
FEB 1
PM
Japan

PAR A
AIR

d Morning, Goldie!

es the "WR/gf" at the bottom of
ally's letters mean he's still mak-
ng you type all his correspondence?
o me a favor, would you? Remind Mr.
uss that I said I'd be happy to an-
wer any questions he has regarding the fountain so long as
he writes to me himself. (He can
use my U.S. address. I have all my
mail forwarded to me when I travel.)
You have an aquarium, don't you,
Goldie? I'm sending along some
friends to keep you company in
your office -- koi, fantails, black
mollies and (of course!) gold fish.
I'll bring more for the fountain.

Sayonara, Goldie! Florence

Gold
Dri
Dr
U.

DRY CREEK MIDDLE SCHOOL

M E M O

DATE: FEBRUARY 22

TO: GOLDIE FISCH

FR: PRINCIPAL WALTER RUSS

RE: THE FOUNTAIN

Haven't I told you repeatedly how important it is for you to deliver priority correspondence to me in a timely manner? I distinctly remember asking you to transcribe and send a letter to Ms. Waters requesting a proposal and bid for the fountain. That was well over a week ago. Surely Ms. Waters has responded by now.

I'll expect her correspondence on my desk when I return from my hair appointment. I trust you DID remember to take care of THAT.

Mr. Russ,

As I told you, sir, Florence has asked that you write to her yourself to request the information you need regarding the fountain. She feels that given your education, you should be responsible for your own correspondence. (I tend to agree.)

You have a 2:00 appointment at the Curl and Twirl.

Sincerely,
Goldie Fisch

THE DRY CREEK GAZETTE
"The Creek May Be Dry, But the Gossip Is Juicy!"
Established 1897

ruary 23rd Edition

35 Cents

Curl And Twirl Snarls Another Victim

What locals are now calling Dry Creek's
"ir Scare" continued yesterday, claiming yet
ther victim.

After requesting a simple trim of his mus-
e, Middle School Principal Walter Russ left
rl's Curl and Twirl in a snarl.

One witness described the scene this way:
oked like old Walter had a dead squirrel
ck on his face."

Another witness disagreed. "I'd say it
ked more like two dead squirrels were hang-
out of his mouth."

Principal Walter Russ could not be reached
comment about the condition of his mus-
he. According to his secretary, Russ
rned from the hair salon, grumbled some-
g unintelligible, and then locked himself in
office.

PRINCIPAL RUSS
(Photo courtesy of Paddy)

As she has in the past, Curl and Twirl
owner Pearl O. Ster blamed the mishap on the
local water supply.

"I'm about ready to throw in my towel tur-
ban," said a despondent Ster, who has operated
the Curl and Twirl for 47 years. "I never used
to have these problems back when I could wash
my customers' hair with spring water, straight
from the tap. You just can't get water pressure
like that from a bottle."

Unnamed sources suggest Ster's age could
be at the root of her problem.

"Well, that's true, too," Ster conceded.
"I'm not as young as I used to be. Maybe I'll
just have to retire. But I still say it's this dang
bottled water that's causing all the problems.
Look around. Everyone's got bad hair in Dry
Creek now. It's the lack of water pressure."

Fisher Cutbait, a favorite Dry Creek bar-
ber, agreed with Ster.

"She's right," Cutbait said. "This is a bad
hair town. Has been for 30 years. Most of my
customers wear hats."

PRINCIPAL RUSS
(Composite sketch courtesy of Lily)

Ms. Florence Waters
Flowing Waters Fountains, Etc.

February 23

Ms. Waters:

I don't think you realize how busy I am, especially now
with this matter of the fountain.

All I'm asking from you is this:

1) a cost estimate for a simple, modest, no-non-
   sense drinking fountain, and

2) a design plan for same.

I fail to see why this information is so difficult to obtain.
I also wonder how you get any work done when you're
always off gallivanting around the globe.

I ask that you respond at once to my attention. And
please remember, Ms. Waters: This is, after all, just a
fountain.

Harshly,

Walter Russ

Mr. Walter Russ
Principal

Florence, Italy
March 1

Dear Wally Russ,

JUST a fountain?

I beg your humble pardon, sir. Are we talking about the same thing here? Are we on the same page? A fountain of water, correct?

Did you not learn in school that water is the source of all life? Were you not paying attention when your teacher told you that water covers 70 percent of the entire planet?

Don't tell me you were busy passing MEMOS to other students, were you? Hmmmmmmmm? You were? I had my hunches.

Let me take this opportunity to refresh your memory and tell you that water makes up 75 percent of the human body. The human brain is 80 percent water. Cabbage, my dear man, is 92.4 percent water.

My fountains are a celebration of the life force, a tribute to tributaries, a praise of waves, a fanciful *fiesta de fluidas*.

JUST a fountain? Indeed not.

Oh yes, you wanted to know what the fountain will look like. Here's your answer: Remember the bulletin board in Mr. Sam N.'s classroom? The one with all of the children's ideas for the fountain? Well, my fountain will look nothing like any one of those drawings, but a little like all of them.

Cost estimate? Less than a gazillion lira.

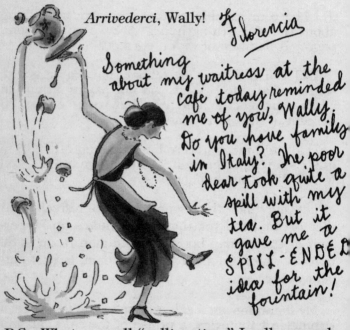

Arrivederci, Wally! *Florencia*

Something about my waitress at the café today reminded me of you, Wally. Do you have family in Italy? The poor dear took quite a spill with my tea. But it gave me a SPILL-ENDED idea for the fountain!

P.S. What you call "gallivanting," I call research.

P.P.S. See you at Dry Creek Days. I'm coming to unveil the new fountain.

March 9

Ms. Florence Waters
President
Flowing Waters Fountains, Etc.

Ms. Waters,

Unveil the new fountain? There seems to be a misunderstanding.

The school board has not approved the new drinking fountain. Frankly, given Sally Mander's fierce opposition to the matter, I wouldn't be surprised if the project is shelved until at least next year.

As you know, Ms. Waters, we have not yet received the proper paperwork from you to authorize the purchase of a new drinking fountain. (I did see some architectural drawings on Goldie's desk last week. She said they were your sketches for the fountain, but surely these were in jest.)

All of which is to say this whole matter is still very much up in the air. Therefore, you should not under any circumstance make plans to install the new drinking fountain until you receive official approval from me.

Officially,

Walter Russ

Mr. Walter (not WALLY) Russ
Principal

... good news! It looks like I'll have your new fountain ready by the end of May, just in time
for Drug Creek Days!

But first, I have a favor to ask of you.
To go with all my fountains, I'd like to tie this
one into the nearest natural water source:
So you know where that might be in Drug Creek?

Ideally, I'd like to connect the fountain to the nearest
babbling brook, creek, spring or stream, that
ways I can circulate clear, fresh water through
the fountain.

I know the famous Spring Creek dried up long
ago, but surely there's a brook or stream some-
where nearby. I'm guessing that in putting
together your history of Drug Creek, you might
have stumbled across a topographical map
of the town. Yes? If so, would you please
send it to me? Gracias, amigos! Hasta la vista, Florence

To: Fifth Grade Class
Drug Creek Middle School
Drug Creek, MO
U.S.A.

P.S. Isn't this butterfly amazing?
It's called a Blue Morpho.
I'm sending one with this
card. Will living many more
with me when I come to
Drug Creek. Won't they look
marvelous fluttering a-
round the fountain? Watch
what happens when it flies.

Did you know that butter-
flies taste with their hind
feet?

March 17

Florence,

We love the Blue Morpho butterfly! We all said it's the most beautiful creature any of us has ever seen. **Mr. N. said so, too, but then he said we've never seen Florence Waters. We asked him if we could form a Florence Waters Fan Club and he said only if he could be president for life!**

Lily *and* Paddy

Hi, Florence!

Thanks a million for the cool butterfly you sent us! Mr. N. let us turn off the lights in the classroom so the butterfly could fly free. Its blue wings flash and sparkle. It looked like a flying flashbulb. Or fireworks. Or a shooting star. But you're the real star in my book.

Gil

Florence:
Thank you for the tape recorders. We'll send a tape of the song we're working on along with this letter. The tape recorders are just what we need when we go out on our interviews. Yes, we're STILL working on "The History of Dry Creek," but it's not as boring as we thought it would be. *Especially since Mr. N. lets us out of class to work on it.*

Yours in notes (musical and otherwise),

Tad *and Shelly*

Dear Florence,
How can we ever thank you for your wonderful gifts? I'm beginning to worry that the corn dogs and cotton candy we plan to serve you at Dry Creek Days aren't going to come even close to thanking you properly. Well, the least we can do is find the topographical map you need. We'll send it along as soon as we find it.

Your friend,

Minnie O.

DRY CREEK WATER COMPANY

"Where Clean Water Is A 'D-EEL!'"

Bringing You the Very Best Water for 30 Years

Delbert "Dee" Eel
President

PRIVATE

March 19

Sal,

Trouble with a capital "T."

When I was at school this morning mopping up the overflow from the drinking fountain, I ran into a pack of fifth graders.

They asked me if I knew anything about natural water sources in Dry Creek. Seems the wacko they've hired to install the new fountain wants to tie into a fresh water source.

I don't like this, Sally. Not one bit. If the people in this town find out what's under . . . . Well, let's just say we're going to be washed up, so to speak.

We need to talk. Fast. The "leak" is getting worse all the time. I'm beginning to wish we never dammed this river city.

Dee

P.S. And what's the deal with the kids at this school, anyway? They used to be so quiet and well-behaved. Now they're bouncing around like a bunch of jumping beans — laughing, dancing, wearing hats and capes and parading around in a marching band. They even have a couple of monkeys running around with them! One of the little beasts (kids, not monkeys) told me the fountain designer is sending them all this stuff. Is that legal?

70

DRY CREEK SWIMMING POOL

FAX

March 20
7:20 A.M.

TO: Dee Eel
President
Dry Creek Water Co.

FR: Sally Mander
Chief Executive Officer
Dry Creek Swimming Pool

RE: Monkey business

Dee,

I don't like it either.

Time to batten down the hatches. I'm calling an emergency meeting tonight of all school board members.

Meeting starts at 6:30. Come early so we can discuss strategy.

READ AND DESTROY

S.M.

END OF TRANSMISSION

A JEWEL OF A POOL

Hi, Florence!

We took our tape recorders to the school board meeting last night. Since they were talking about you, we thought you might get a kick out of seeing some of the transcripts.

Mander: "Mr. Russ, I have learned from reliable sources that you are proceeding with plans to install a spanking new drinking fountain in Dry Creek Middle School. Where is the purchase order for this capital expenditure? Where is the approval from the school board? By what authority have you approved this acquisition?

"Are you aware, Mr. Russ, that you are currently in violation of School Board Rule 1322 - APOWFWPAFPA - Approving Purchase Of Water Facility Without Proper Authority From Proper Authorities? Yes, you are treading on thin ice, Mr. Russ!"

Russ: "Er, uh, yes, well . . . But did you know that water is the source of life? Seventy percent—"

Mander: "What's this fountain going to look like? How much is it going to cost? Why haven't other bids been considered? There's no room for secrets in a democracy! This thing could cost a fortune for all we know! And you expect the taxpayers in our community to pay for this? Without a vote of the people? Where I come from that's called taxation without representation! And who is this Florence Waters character, anyway?"

Russ: "Well, she has something of an artistic bent, but—"

Mander: "I'll tell you what she is. She's nutty as a fruitcake! By exposing the students of Dry Creek to this wacko, Walter Russ, you are endangering the hearts and minds of our children, not to mention turning them into a band of unruly urchins. Monkeys in the classroom? This is an outrage! Never in my 30 years of service as school board president have I seen such a disgrace! I hope you know I intend to go to *The Dry Creek Gazette* with this story. And by the way, Walter, consider your pool pass revoked!"

Florence: We think you're the greatest. Sally Mander is the one who's nutty. Only eight weeks till Dry Creek Days! See ya then!

The 5th-grade urchins

Tad Lily Gil Minnie
Paddy Shelly

THE DRY CREEK GAZETTE

"The Creek May Be Dry, But the Gossip Is Juicy!"

Established 1897

March 22nd Edition

35 Cents

SALLY MANDER

Sally Mander Accuses Principal Of Slippery Practices; Says Florence Waters Is Bribing Students, Faculty

An emergency meeting of the Dry Creek School Board was called Wednesday night by Sally Mander. Ms. Mander is organizing a campaign to "Save Our Old Fountain" (SOOF) and "Dump Wacko Fountain Lady" (DWFL).

Mander says she is "outraged" that Principal Walter Russ is proceeding with plans to install a new drinking fountain in the middle school.

"We haven't even voted on it!" exclaimed Ms. Mander, who called Russ' *(Continued on page 2, column 1)*

Hair Scare Continues To Tease Dry Creek

After a bad shampoo and cut, another Curl and Twirl customer says she won't be back.

"It's just terrible what that woman did to my hair," said Ima Crabbie, a longtime customer of the Curl and Twirl beauty salon.

Crabbie was last seen wearing an oversized hunting cap on her head. Witnesses reported hearing Crabbie tell friends, "I'm not taking this hat off until my hair grows out."

Curl and Twirl owner Pearl O. Ster maintains the recent hair crisis is not her fault. But unnamed sources report that authorities will close the Curl and Twirl if the problem is not resolved.

IMA CRABBIE

74

rom page 1)

ions an example of his "flagrant disregard
the democratic process."

Mander also objects to the proposed con-
ctor for the project. According to Mander,
untain designer Florence Waters has sent
pensive gifts to the students of Dry Creek
ddle School.

"Isn't it obvious that she's trying to bribe
e students and faculty of Dry Creek Middle
hool?" Mander asked the school board mem-
rs. "Never in my thirty years in Dry Creek
ve I seen such an obvious and pathetic ploy.
ll me old-fashioned, but I can't believe
meone would try to win the affection of our
ildren with gifts. As long as I'm school
ard president, the students of Dry Creek are
t for sale!"

When asked, Principal Walter Russ
knowledged that no invoices have been
ceived for the many gifts sent to the school
Ms. Waters.

Sally Mander believes that instead of
talling a new drinking fountain, taxpayer
llars would be better spent repairing the cur-
nt fountain. She recommended Delbert
ee" Eel for the job.

"Or maybe we could just take the money
d buy everyone in town an ice cream cone,"
s. Mander suggested with a wink.

"For 30 years this fountain has served
our children well. But now, there are
those in our community who wish to
throw it away. Beware, my friends! If
they would discard this lovely old water
fountain, what will be next on their
agenda? Where will it stop? I'll tell you
what they're trying to do -- throw the
babies out with the bathwater. Don't let
them! We must protect our children
from the corruption of the modern age.
That's why I ask for your support in my
campaign to Save Our Old Fountain."
-Sally Mander
Concerned Citizen

From the Desk of
PRINCIPAL WALTER RUSS

From the Desk of
PRINCIPAL WALTER RUSS

ie Desk of
RUSS

DATE __March 23__   HOUR __8:25__
TO __Mr. Walter Russ__

WHILE YOU WERE OUT

Ms. __Annette Trap__
OF __The Dry Creek Gazette__
PHONE __746-4301__

- ☐ Telephoned ☐ Returned Call ☐ Left Package
- ☒ Please Call ☐ Was In ☐ Please See Me
- ☐ Will Call Again ☐ Won't Call ☐ Important

MESSAGE: __A reporter from The Dry Creek Gazette called for a comment about Wednesday night's school board meeting. Please call her back. She said it's regarding the fountain.__

Signed __Goldie F.__

From the Desk of
PRINCIPAL WALTER RUSS

From the Desk of
AL WALTER RUSS

he Desk of

RUSS

DATE March 23   HOUR 10:39
TO Mr. Walter Russ

WHILE YOU WERE OUT
?

M _____
OF _____
PHONE _____

☒ Telephoned ☐ Returned Call ☐ Left Package
☐ Please Call ☐ Was In ☐ Please See Me
☐ Will Call Again ☐ Won't Call ☐ Important

MESSAGE: A woman called to request a donation for the SOOF and DWFL campaigns. (It's regarding the fountain.) The woman wouldn't leave her name or number, but she said she still hasn't received her pool pass back from you.

Signed Goldie F.

77

From the D

PRINCIPAL WALTER RU

From the Desk of

PRINCIPAL WALTER

From

TER

DATE _March 23_ HOUR _1:47_
TO _Mr. Walter Russ_

WHILE YOU WERE OUT

Mr. _Barry Cuda_
OF _Sharks, Sharks and Sharks_
PHONE _1-800-GO4Blood_

☐ Telephoned ☒ Returned Call ☐ Left Package
☒ Please Call ☐ Was In ☐ Please See Me
☐ Will Call Again ☐ Won't Call ☐ Important

MESSAGE: _Barry Cuda, the_
school attorney, return-
ed your call. Please call
him back. Regarding
the fountain.

Signed _Goldie F._

ADVISORY TO ALL STAFF
(Especially Mr. Sam N.)
FROM PRINCIPAL WALTER RUSS

March 24

REGARDING THE FOUNTAIN:

Please be advised that plans to install the new school drinking fountain are officially on hold.

Because of the controversy surrounding the choice of Florence Waters for the project, I am asking for an immediate termination in all communication between our school (students, teachers, administrative staff) and Ms. Waters.

Also, I've been informed by our school attorney, Barry Cuda, that it would be wise at this time to return all gifts sent to the school from Florence Waters.

I expect full and immediate cooperation.

Mr. Walter Russ

FIFTH-GRADE ANNOUNCEMENTS

March 24th

TOMORROW: Field trip to Dry Creek County Courthouse to work on town history.

Important: We've got to return all the gifts* Florence sent us this year. Bring everything back to school. We'll box the stuff up and send it back to Florence.

(I know. I'm sad too.)

Mr. N.

*WORD OF THE DAY: gift. 1. Something given freely and without compensation; a present or donation. 2. A natural talent, endowment, aptitude, or flair.

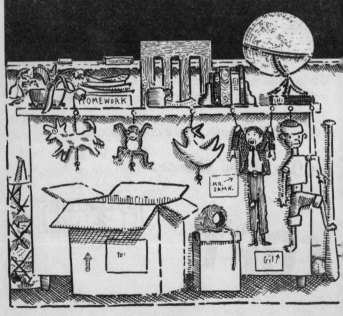

Dear Florence,

Bad news. Make that TERRIBLE news.

We found out yesterday that we can't write to you anymore. We're not even supposed to be writing <u>this</u> letter, but we wanted to tell you why you won't be hearing from us ever again.

It's something about the fight between the principal and the school board president. Not that it makes any difference. All that matters is that we can't write to you anymore or get letters back from you. It's completely unfair.

We're really sorry if we lost you the job of designing the new drinking fountain. We were all so excited to see what it would look like. Mr. N. said he thought the fountain would be "a thing of grace and beauty, like Florence Waters herself." (We really wanted you and Mr. N. to meet, but that's out the window now, too.)

And get this: We have to return all the things you sent us this year. We know you weren't trying to bribe anyone, but try telling that to Sally Mander. (And if she thinks any of us are going to buy passes to swim in her crummy pool this summer, she's got another thought coming.)

Anyway, even though you won't be hearing from us anymore, we'll be thinking of you and missing you.

With love and sadness,

Minnie   Gil   Tad

Lily   Paddy   Shelly

March 25

Flowing Waters Fountains, Etc.
Watertown, CA

Dear Florence,

The kids wanted to break the news to you themselves. I didn't see their letter, but I'm assuming they told you what's going on around here. What a bunch of nonsense, huh? Guess it's time for me to find another line of work. (And believe me: It'll be easier to find another job than to find another pen pal as charming as you.)

We have so enjoyed getting to know you this year. Your letters were the high point of each week. (We always saved them for AFTER the spelling tests.) And your gifts were so much fun to open and wear, or play with, or eat, or just look at . . . .

But most of all we enjoyed you, Florence. We talked about your trips, charting your travels on our map. And we spent many afternoons wondering where you were, what you were doing, what it would be like when we finally met you face-to-face.

Unfortunately, this is where it must end. Not that we'll stop thinking about you, of course. It's just that now we'll never get a chance to tell you in person how much we value your friendship.

Better sign off before I embarrass myself. Please let us know the best way to return the gifts to you.

Fondly,

Sam R.

P.S. For your amusement, I'm enclosing my own design for the new fountain.

me ↗

The Nile River

Sam, you never told me you were an artist! Your drawing was wonderful— and your letter sweet. Apologies from the fifth-grade class completely unnecessary. Will respond to Mr. Ruse and Ms. Mander under separate cover. More importantly: Do you all have scuba gear? What about ice skates? Need to know for the fountain. Also, I'm sending a parcel containing cyperus papyrus. This is the famous Egyptian paper plant. Please plant it in a combination of rich soil and shallow water. I'll transplant it when I arrive. Cheer up, buckies! —Florence

Drug Creek Middle
School
Fifth-grade Class
Drug Creek, MO
U.S.A.

TELL-A-GRAM
The Old-Timey Telegram Company

Sent from: F. Waters
Cairo, Egypt

3:55 A / P M

Sent to: Principal Wally Russ
Dry Creek Middle School
Dry Creek, MO USA

I HAD NO INTENTION OF BILLING YOU FOR THE

THINGS I SENT THE CHILDREN - STOP - AND I

CERTAINLY WASN'T TRYING TO BRIBE ANYONE -

STOP - I WAS CLEANING MY ATTIC FOR GOODNESS

SAKE - STOP - AND THE MONKEYS WERE A GIFT

TO ME FROM AN AFRICAN TRIBE I'VE KNOWN FOR

YEARS - STOP - IF THE ACCUSATIONS AND

ACCUSERS WEREN'T SO SILLY I'D BE INSULTED

- STOP - BUT REALLY — WHO HAS THE TIME -

STOP - IF YOU WISH I WILL PICK UP MY THINGS

PERSONALLY WHEN I COME TO DRY CREEK TO

INSTALL THE NEW FOUNTAIN - STOP —

-FLORENCE

APR 3   P M

Form 1801

April 8

Ms. Florence Waters
Flowing Waters Fountains, Etc.

Ms. Waters:

Install the new fountain?

It seems I am not making myself clear. There isn't going to BE a new fountain, Ms. Waters.

There are those in this community who feel that your involvement with our students is, shall we say, "unhealthy."

We thank you for your time. If we are in need of your services in the future, we will contact you. But given the current climate surrounding this issue, the fountain project is "OFF."

Surely there can be no more confusion on this point.

Walter Russ

Mr. Walter Russ
Principal

Copacabana Beach, Rio de Janeiro

No confusion, indeed.

As you say, the fountain is "OFF." And
I agree: That is unhealthy, especially
in a school full of thirsty children.
But that's why I'm coming to turn
the fountain "ON."

To be honest, Mr. Wally Russ, I'm increasingly concerned about your health.
You know what you need? A nice
vacation. A little sand and between
your toes. So bring a few trunks
full when I come to Dry Creek.
(Full of sand, I mean. Not toes.)

Your friend. Florence

P.S. What does one wear to
Dry Creek I says?

Wally Russ
Princey Pal
Dry Creek Middle
School
Dry Creek, M. O.
U. S. A.

87

The penguin takes only one mate in its life-time. Penguins are such devoted parents, they will starve to death if necessary to provide food for their children.

The swordfish is the fastest fish in the sea. It can swim 68 miles per hour.

An electric eel can produce a shock of more than 600 volts. Though it is born with eyes, the eel is blind as an adult. It uses its electricity to find food.

The lanternfish has phosphorescent light organs which act as a miner's lamp when the fish is swimming in dark waters. Studies have shown that when confined to an aquarium, the lanternfish's "lamp" can provide enough light to allow a person to read in an otherwise dark room.

The garfish has green bones.

Sea lions can swim 6,000 miles, stopping only to sleep. At one time there were more sea lions on earth than people.

The *white shark* lives in a state of continual hunger. No matter how much it eats, it is never satisfied.

The *starfish* is the only animal able to turn its stomach inside out.

Some *salmon* are able to leap 15 feet high.

The *herring* is the most widely eaten fish in the world. A *red herring* is a smoked herring OR a device used to draw attention from the matter or issue at hand.

Flamingoes are not naturally pink. They derive their unique coloring from their diet of tiny blue-green algae which turn pink in the digestive process.

A *marine catfish* can taste with any part of its body.

Dry Creek Middle School
Dry Creek, Missouri
"We Thirst for Knowledge"

April 14

Dear Florence,

I know I shouldn't be writing to you. Principal Russ has asked me not to. But I did something today I've never done before, and you're the only person I can tell.

As you can imagine, we were all terribly upset by the principal's decision to ban all communication between the school and you. But no one was more disappointed than Mr. Sam N. Today he submitted his resignation. I just couldn't believe it. Mr N. is the best teacher in this school. The kids absolutely love him.

Well, Mr. N. put the official resignation form in the principal's mailbox. And, Florence, before I knew what I was doing, I stole it! The resignation form, I mean. I didn't know what to do with it or where to put it, so I'm sending it to you for safekeeping.

Florence, as I said, I've never done anything like this before. If anyone finds out, I could lose my job.

Did I do the right thing?

Goldi q

OFFICIAL RESIGNATION FORM

I, _____*Sam R.*_____ hereby submit my
resignation from the position of _*fifth-grade teacher*_
for reason(s) described below:

_____

_____

_____*Creative differences with*_____
_____*school administration*_____

_____

_____

_____

_____

_____

My resignation shall be effective

*at the end of current school year.*

Signature_____*Sam R.*_____

Date_____*April 14*_____

DRY CREEK MIDDLE SCHOOL

April 14

Dearest Florence,

I shouldn't be writing to you. Principal Russ
has asked me not to. But somehow, Florence,
you inspire me to break the rules. Besides, looking over some of your old letters (my favorite
form of entertainment these days), I realize that
we neglected to respond to a specific question
you asked. Surely Mr. Russ can't fault me for
being polite, can he?

Scuba gear and ice skates? No, Florence, the
students have neither. I hesitate to ask what
you have in mind. But please remember, we can
no longer accept your very generous gifts. In
fact, we've spent the last couple of weeks pack-
ing up the things you've sent us this year. Not
surprisingly, the kids are having a hard time.
We're just thankful we don't have to return your
letters. *That* would be unbearable.

I don't suppose you still plan to come here
for Dry Creek Days. Now that the fountain project has been called to a halt, I guess there's
really no reason for you to make the trip. I can
assure you that your presence will be missed
even more than your presents.

Thinking of you more than you know,

Sam M.

Dry Creek Middle School
Dry Creek, MO

April 14
Dear Florence,

We know we're not allowed to write to you anymore, but we wanted to let you know that we really wish you'd still come for Dry Creek Days. Our band is going to play a few songs. After that, we have to send the instruments back to you. The principal is only letting us perform at Dry Creek Days because we've been practicing so long. This is the biggest drag in the world.

Tad *and Shelly*

April 14

Hi, Florence.

I'm not supposed to write to you, but I feel so terrible about everything that's happening around here lately. It's such a mess. And now we've got to send back all the things you've sent us this year. It's so unfair.

And, Florence, I feel so terrible but I think I lost one of the tape recorders you sent. I can't find it anywhere. I just know I'm going to get in huge trouble. I miss you, Florence, even though I've never met you. I wish you'd come for Dry Creek Days.

Minnie O.

Dear Florence,

We're not supposed to send letters to you any-more, but we wanted to let you know that we've looked everywhere and still can't find the topographical map you asked us to send. We checked the records at the Dry Creek County Courthouse. The map was checked out of the county library 30 years ago by Dee-Sal Builders, Inc., the construction company that built the school. Guess they forgot to return the map to the library when they finished.

One good thing came out of our search for the map. When we were at the courthouse, we found a folder full of old newspaper clippings about Dry Creek, back when it was still called Spring Creek. It's good reference material for our town history project, though we've kind of lost interest in that whole thing — unless of course you're still planning to come see the performance. Are you?

2.

We're going to present our "History of Dry Creek" report at Dry Creek Days. Well, we will if we get finished in time. There's so much stuff to read. Some of it's kind of interesting. We'll enclose a couple of the old newspaper clippings we found over at the courthouse. The articles are super old — 30 years to be exact. The paper even had a different name back then. You might recognize some of the people mentioned in the articles. Weird, huh?

We miss you, Florence, and hope you'll come see us in May.

Lily

Paddy

Gil

THE SPRING CREEK GAZETT

"The Creek May Be Wet, But Our Ink Is Dry!"

Established 1897

February 4th Edition   10

Sally Mander Wins School Board Electi
"New Middle School Now!"

SALLY MANDER AND DELBERT

In celebrating her victory, Sally M
repeated her campaign pledge. "It's time t
a modern middle school!" said Ms. Mand
newly elected school board president.

"The current school is a disgrace," co
Mander, co-owner of Dee-Sal Builders, Inc
need to build a new school — and fast!"

Ms. Mander has drafted blueprints for t
posed school. Contrary to past practices at
Creek Middle School, Mander is refusing
sider other designs for the school building.

"The people of Spring Creek have sp
Mander said. "My election is a mandate t
the school as I see fit. Anyone who disagr
go soak his head in the spring!"

The new school will be constructed by
"Dee" Eel, co-owner of Dee-Sal Builder
Ms. Mander and Mr. Eel moved to Spring
earlier this year.

Pearl O. Ster: Beautician of the Year (AGAI

In an announcement that surprised no one, Pearl O. Ster has been named Beautician of the Year for the 15th year in a row.

"Thank you so much," the grateful Ster said, "but the award really belongs to the wonderful spring water in this town, without which I would be up a creek without a blow-dryer."

Today's Lunch Special at the
Spring Creek Cafe
Aunt Joan's Salmon Cakes with dill sauce

PEARL O. STER ACCEPTS AWAR

96

HE SPRING CREEK GAZETTE
"The Creek May Be Wet, But Our Ink Is Dry!"
Established 1897

:h 15th Edition   10 Cents

esign For New Middle School Kept Secret; ander Promises "Wonderful Surprise"

ALLY MANDER AND DELBERT "DEE" EEL

In a press conference this morning, Sally Mander defended her decision to keep secret her plans for the new Spring Creek Middle School.

"Don't you people understand the importance of secrets?" asked Mander. "Children love surprises. That's why my construction foreman, Dee Eel, and I have decided to keep the design a secret."

According to Mander, construction of the new school will be complete by late May.

"We're planning a grand unveiling for Spring Creek Days," Mander said. Delbert Eel then reportedly began to giggle uncontrollably. "I'll say it'll be grand!" he said. "Thirty grand for us!"

At that, Sally Mander stepped on Eel's foot. According to witnesses standing nearby, Mander whispered angrily to Eel: "Why can't you keep your big mouth shut? You're going to give the whole thing away!"

As the press conference ended, Sally Mander encouraged those in attendance to value the childlike pleasures in everyday life.

"We could all do well to look to the children as an example," said Mander. "They're so looking forward to the unveiling of their new school. For the children's sake, let's not spoil the surprise."

PARIS

April 23

Dry Creek Middle School
Fifth-Grade Class
Dry Creek, MO USA

Mes cheris,

OF COURSE I'm still planning to attend Dry Creek Days. Do you think I'd pass up a chance to see the first public performance by Sam N.'s Tune-A-Combo? And how could I miss hearing "The History of Dry Creek" as presented by the historians of the fifth-grade class?

I was intrigued by the old newspaper clippings you sent. Pearl O. Ster sounds lovely, as do Ms. Mander and Mr. Eel. Have you interviewed them for your town history report?

I've found some glorious things here in France for the fountain. Swans are essential, don't you agree? All that's left now is to locate a natural water source in Dry Creek. Not to worry. Something will come up, I'm sure.

I'm enclosing some chocolates from Paris. Enjoy! And please deliver the gift-wrapped box of candies to Goldie Fisch.

Au revoir!

P.S. I always stay at the Hotel Fontaine when I'm in Paris. *Fontaine* means "fountain" in French. Paris is the setting of one of my favorite novels, *Les Misérables*, written by the French author Victor Hugo. The best scene in the book takes place in the city sewers. Incredible, no? I'll send a copy of the novel along with the chocolates.

HOTEL FONTAINE

You did the right thing, Goldie.
Florence

DRY CREEK WATER COMPANY

"Where Clean Water Is A 'D-EEL!'"
Bringing You the Very Best Water for 30 Years

Delbert "Dee" Eel
President

May 6

Sally,

Listen to this: Some kids from the middle school showed up at my office this morning. The brats wanted to interview ME for the town history they're working on. Lots of questions about WHEN the creek dried up and WHY. Of course I played dumb. The little rugrats can't make ME talk.

Then they wanted to know if I had any topographical maps of this area. As if I'm going to let those monkeys in on the best-kept secret in town. I let them take a picture of me in my office. Then I told them to scram.

But here's the real problem: The "leak" around the base of the fountain is getting worse every day. I'm telling you, Sally, it was practically gushing this morning. You gotta see this thing. Come over to school so I can show you what I mean.

URGENT

Dee

DRY CREEK SWIMMING POOL

CRYSTAL-CLEAR ALL YEAR   TEMPERATURE-CONTROLLED   YEAR-ROUND FUN

....

FAX

May 7
4:20 P.M.

FOR YOUR EYES ONLY

TO: Dee Eel
President
Dry Creek Water Co.

FR: Sally Mander
Chief Executive Officer
Dry Creek Swimming Pool

RE: The fountain

Gushing?

I'll stop by school on my way to work tomorrow morning. Meet me at the fountain at 7:30 A.M. *Sal*

P.S. Don't worry about the kids. They photographed me earlier today, too. Little savages, aren't they? I shut them up by giving them all ice cream. You've got to learn how to handle kids, Dee.

....

A JEWEL OF A POOL

102

Florence: Have we got news for you! Minnie O. found the missing tape recorder this morning. It was in her locker, which is right next to the drinking fountain. She must have left the recorder turned on because when we played the tape back this morning, this is what we heard:

VOICE 1: "See what I mean, Sal?"

VOICE 2: "Good heavens! Look at that leak!"

VOICE 1: "I'm telling ya, Sal. It's worse than ever."

VOICE 2: "What the devil is going on, Dee?"

VOICE 1: "Got me. For some reason, the spring is getting stronger all the—"

VOICE 2: "Shhhhhhh!"

VOICE 1: "What?"

VOICE 2: "STOP using that word!"

VOICE 1: "What word? 'Spring'?"

VOICE 2: "Shhhhhh! Do you want someone to hear you?"

VOICE 1: "Who's gonna hear me, Sal?"

VOICE 2: "Anyone could hear your big mouth."

VOICE 1: "Who are you saying has a big mouth?"

VOICE 2: "Delbert Eel, that's who. Now hush up before you tell the whole world there's a natural spring under this drinking fountain .... What was that? I hear somebody coming. Look busy."

Pretty fishy, wouldn't you agree? Looks like we've found a natural water source for you AND an intriguing plot twist for our "History of Dry Creek."

The 5th-Grade Detective Agency

TELL-A-GRAM
The Old-Timey Telegram Company

Sent from: F. Waters
Waterdown, Ontario CANADA 10:02 A P M

Sent to: Fifth-Grade Detective Agency
Dry Creek Middle School
Dry Creek, MO USA

BRILLIANT - STOP - ARRIVING ON THE 24TH -

STOP - CAN TASTE THE COTTON CANDY ALREADY

- STOP - SEE YOU SOON - STOP —

FLORENCE

'MAY 1 5 A.M.

Form 1801

104

YOU ARE INVITED

Come one, Come all
to the annual celebration of
Dry Creek Days!

This year's activities include
the annual Dry Creek Parade
and Carnival

PLUS

A Special Musical Presentation
by
Sam N.'s Tune-A-Combo

AND

"The History Of Dry Creek":

The Riveting Saga Of
Our Fair City

As Narrated By
the Fifth-Grade Class

AND

The Grand Unveiling of the
New Drinking Fountain
in the Middle School!

THE DRY CREEK GAZETTE

"The Creek May Be Dry, But the Gossip Is Juicy!"

Established 1897

May 22nd Edition   35 Cents

DRY CREEK DAYS HERE AGAIN!
Fifth-Grade Class Promises "Big Surprise"

FIFTH GRADERS AT MIDDLE SCHOOL:
(LEFT TO RIGHT) GIL, SHELLY, PADDY,
MINNIE, TAD, LILY

Just two days before Dry Creek Days celebrations are scheduled to begin, the fifth-grade class at Dry Creek Middle School called a press conference to make an announcement.

"Our class has uncovered some information we think you'll all be interested to hear," class spokesperson Minnie O. said.

"It involves the town of Dry Creek and the people who live here," Minnie continued.

When asked if the information was good news or bad news, members of the class whispered among themselves. "Both," they finally replied in unison.

"But that's all we can say for now," Minnie concluded. "You'll have to come to Dry Creek Days. We'll tell you the whole story then."

Fountain Designer to Arrive by Train Day after Tomorrow

Florence Waters, president of Flowing Waters Fountains, Etc., is scheduled to arrive in Dry Creek on Friday by private rail car.

"I can't possibly fit everything in my suitcases," Waters wrote in a letter to the Dry Creek depot, explaining her reason for traveling with 17 freight cars in addition to her private coach.

"I'm bringing a few doodads and gewgaws with me," Waters wrote to depot officials. "Just a few things I've picked up during my travels. I think they'll look nice on the new water fountain."

Waters plans to install the new school drinking fountain during Dry Creek Days.

DRY CREEK DEPOT

M E M O

DATE: MAY 22

TO: GOLDIE FISCH

FR: PRINCIPAL WALTER RUSS

RE: THE FOUNTAIN

There was an error in today's paper regarding the installation of a new fountain. Get the editor of *The Dry
Creek Gazette* on the phone for me so I can demand a
retraction.

*Mr. Russ,
The editor stands by the
story in today's paper
regarding the fountain.
Goldie Fisch*

FIFTH-GRADE ANNOUNCEMENTS

May 22nd

ASSIGNMENTS:

"History of Dry Creek"

> Final draft due tomorrow
> Dress rehearsal Friday morning
> Are we ready for this?
> *(Are they ready for this?)*

Band practice: 1:10 p.m.

WORD OF THE DAY: Gewgaw.

This is a word Florence used to describe the things she's bringing for the fountain. Will somebody please look it up in the dictionary and post the page on the bulletin board?

Thanks.   Mr. N.

gew•gaw *n.* An ornamental trinket or bauble.

gey•ser *n.* A natural hot spring that periodically spouts a column of water and steam into the air.

ghast•ly *adj.* Terrifying; dreadful. Morally shocking.

geyser

DRY CREEK WATER COMPANY

"Where Clean Water Is A 'D-EEL!'"
Bringing You the Very Best Water for 30 Years

Delbert "Dee" Eel
President

May 23

Sally,

Did you see the newspaper yesterday? It looks like they're really going through with plans to pull out our fountain. If so, we need to get in there first and cap off the you-know-what. I think I've got a clamp that's big enough to do the trick. I'll need your help, though. Let's plan on 11 o'clock Friday night. It's late, I know, but at least no one will be around school at that hour.

P.S. The school might be wasting its money on Florence what's-her-name. Looks like the darn you-know-what is ready to burst on its own. This morning I heard a gurgling noise under the fountain followed by a jet of steam. I don't know what's going on down there.

P.P.S. Speaking of what's-her-name, what's the deal with her bringing a trainload of equipment for this job? I can fit a drinking fountain in the back of my truck.

DRY CREEK SWIMMING POOL

CRYSTAL-CLEAR ALL YEAR   TEMPERATURE-CONTROLLED   YEAR-ROUND FUN

FAX

May 24
9:35 A.M.

READ AND DESTROY

TO: Dee Eel
President
Dry Creek Water Co.

FR: Sally Mander
Chief Executive Officer
Dry Creek Swimming Pool

RE: The fountain

It's a date. Tonight. Eleven o'clock p.m. We'll meet at the fountain.

S.M

CONFIDENTIAL

**FOR YOUR
EYES ONLY**

END OF TRANSMISSION

A JEWEL OF A POOL

DRY CREEK INN
DRY CREEK, MISSOURI

5/24

De...
Sam...

Tha...
stop...
tion...
trave...

I...
be rea...
I'm fr...
in join...
details...

The...
hotel...
too. We...

Look...

DATE _May 24_   HOUR _11:20_

TO _Sam N's Fifth-Grade Class_

WHILE YOU WERE OUT

Ms. _Florence Waters_

of _@ Dry Creek Inn_

PHONE _Cre-K Inn_

☐ Telephoned ☐ Returned Call ☐ Left Package
☐ Please Call ☒ Was In ☐ Please See Me!
☐ Will Call Again ☐ Won't Call ☒ Important!

MESSAGE: _Florence Waters is in town! She stopped by to see your class, but you were all out rehearsing for tomorrow's performance. She left a note (see attached)._

Signed _Goldie F._

DRY CREEK INN
DRY CREEK, MISSOURI

5/24

Dear Gil, Tad, Shelly, Minnie, Lily, Paddy, and Sam N.:

The flowers in my hotel room are lovely. Thank you! I'm so sorry I missed you when you stopped by to drop them off. I was at the train station unloading the railcars. (When will I learn to travel light?)

I still have a few loose ends to tie up before I'll be ready to turn on the new fountain tomorrow. I'm free tonight, though. Might you be interested in joining me for dinner? I'd like to discuss a few details with you all regarding the fountain.

There's a lovely restaurant right next to my hotel. Shall we say 7:00? Please invite Goldie, too. We'll make it a Dry Creek Days Eve party.

Looking forward to meeting you all – in person!

Florena

113

TO: Florence Waters
      Guest, Room 257
      Dry Creek Inn

HAND-DELIVERED

May 24
Friday, 4:00 P.M.

Dear Florence,

    Here you are in town, and
we're still communicating by
letter (Sigh). No matter. We'll
see you soon enough when we
dine together tonight at the Dry
Creek Cafe. May I be the first
to recommend the meatloaf
sandwich? The grilled cheese
sandwich is good, too.

        See you in a few hours.

            Nervously,

                Sam

114

DRY CREEK CAFE

TABLE	DATE	TIME	SERVER
2+3	5-24	7:00	Angel

7	grilled cheese	
2	meat loaf sand-	
9	F F	
all	CHiPS	
2	root beer	
3	choc. shakes	
2	Milks	
1	coffee	
1	hot tea (extra H₂0)	
9	slices of Mile. High Dry Creek Pie	

Thank You!   Come Again!

EMERGENCY DISPATCH
DRY CREEK FIRE DEPARTMENT
Fire Marshal: Whitey Bass

DATE: <u>May 24th</u>

TIME: <u>11:36 p.m.</u>

Emergency unit needed immediately at Dry Creek Middle School!

Water flooding first floor of school. Possible break in water main. No reported injuries.

Witnesses (named below) were walking home from a Dry Creek Days Eve party at the Dry Creek Cafe. They reported seeing Delbert "Dee" Eel and Sally Mander running from the middle school. Mander was heard shouting the following at Eel:

"You idiot! I thought you said you could put a clamp on it and shut it off!"

Eel was heard to reply: "Oh yeah? You try shutting it off! That water's dang hot!"

Mander then reportedly said: "Be quiet and let me think! Now wait a minute. I've got an idea. Call the newspaper. We'll hold a press conference in the morning. This just might work."

<u>Witnesses:</u>
Sam N.
Minnie, Gil, Lily, Paddy, Shelly, Tad
Goldie Fisch
Florence Waters

THE DRY CREEK GAZETTE

"The Creek May Be Dry, But the Gossip Is Juicy!"

Established 1897

May 25th Late Edition

35 Cents

SPECIAL DRY CREEK DAYS EDITION

Dry Creek Days: All Washed Up? No Way, Students Say

"It's sad but true," Sally Mander said this morning, the first day of what should be Dry Creek Days. "I'm afraid we're going to have to cancel the celebration this year."

The reason? A broken water main in the Dry Creek Middle School.

"Don't worry," said Mander, smiling. "We'll take care of everything. I've got Delbert Eel working on the problem even as we speak."

Mander, who urged the disappointed crowd to "Run along home now," promised that next year's celebration will be bigger and better than ever before.

But some in the crowd refused to leave. One of those gathered, a fifth-grade student at Dry Creek Middle School, tape-recorded the spirited exchange between Mander and the angry mob.

Minnie: "We're not going anywhere, Ms. Mander, until we tell the people of this town the truth about you and Mr. Eel."

Gil: "That's right. We've spent all year researching the history of Dry Creek."

Lily: "You mean, Spring Creek."

Shelly: "Yeah, it's Spring Creek, 'cause the creek never dried up at all. You and Mr. Eel just made that up so

ANGRY CROWD AT MIDDLE SCHOOL

Curl And Twirl To Close This Weekend

Pearl O. Ster, owner of Pearl's Curl and Twirl, will retire this weekend, bringing an end to what she calls "30 years of bad-hair days."

In her earlier days as a beautician, Ster won countless awards for her special spring water shampoo and scalp treatments. Since the spring dried up, however, such services

(Continued on page 2, column 1)

(Continued on page 2, column 2)

(From page 1)

you could —"

Sally M.: "Children, children! What fanciful imaginations you have! Why don't you prepare a play to perform for us next year during Dry Creek Days?"

Sam N.: "Actually, Ms. Mander, the students have quite a drama to present *this* year. They've even written an opera to accompany it."

Paddy: "Goldie Fisch made costumes for us."

Tad: "And Florence came all this way to install the new drinking fountain."

Walter R.: "New what?"

Minnie: "I vote we proceed with the activities scheduled for Dry Creek Days."

Students: "Hear! Hear!"

Gil: "Let's meet at school tomorrow afternoon at two o'clock. We'll tell the whole town the TRUE history of Dry Creek. After that, Florence can unveil the new fountain she's designed for the school."

Walter R.: "New fountain? But I don't have the paperwork for a new fountain. There can be no capital spending until I get the proper—"

Goldie F.: "Oh, put a lid on it,Wally."

Walter R.: "Ms. Fisch!!"

Reporter: "Ms. Waters, will the break in the water main affect your plans to install the new fountain?"

Florence: "Oh, yes indeed! Isn't it wonderful?"

(From page 1)

were not available. Moreover, Ster's clients have become increasingly dissatisfied with her ability to meet their hair-care needs.

DRY CREEK FLORIST

DATE: May 26	TIME: 10:10 AM
TO: Florence Waters	
ADDRESS: c/o Dry Creek Inn	
FROM: Sam N.	

1 dozen tulips   16.00
+ delivery   2.00
              $18.00

Happy Dry Creek Days,
Florence.
May I escort you to the festivities?

Sam

MAY 26 A.M.

CK # _6012_

THE HISTORY OF DRY CREEK

A Historical Opera

*Written and Performed
by the
Fifth-Grade Class*

(Enter, the CHORUS)

Animato **(with animation)**

Hold on to your hats, folks.
Don't move from your seats.
We're about to tell you
A tale of two cheats.

You know who they are,
You've seen both their faces.
They've lived in this town,
And for years they've disgraced us.

Their names are familiar:
Sal Mander and Dee Eel.
They're partners in crime,
And in companies that steal.

Dee owns the water company,
Sally owns the pool.
But their real business
Is right here in this school.

Here's how their scam works
How they made all their dough.
It's a little complicated,
So we'll take it slow.

Doloroso (sorrowful)

It happened in May,
Thirty years ago,
When people were still able
To watch the creek flow.

Those were the days
When water was free
For drinking and swimming
And making iced tea.

Remember those happy days
When folks always smiled,
And people who moved here
Came for the lifestyle?

Well, we know two folks
Who came to this town
With plans to make
Enough money to drown.

"What this town needs," they said,
"Is a new Middle School.
Let us build it for you;
We'll make it modern and cool."

What they didn't tell us,
What nobody knew,
Is that Sally and Delbert
Are crooks through and through.

Oh sure, they built a new school;
Not a soul in town fussed.
But when the school doors opened,
The creek turned to dust.

It wasn't a coincidence!
It wasn't just fate!
It was part of their plan,
Their plot of greed and hate.

They built the new school
On the source of the spring,
And because of this,
They owned everything.

They capped off the spring,
They rerouted the flow.
They built pipes underground
To move water just so:

We had to pay Dee for water.
We paid Sal to swim.
There was no creek to play in;
The whole town was grim.

Allegro giocoso (**quickly, merrily**)

But do not despair,
Ye citizens of Dry Creek!
The past is behind us,
And now, a new day, a new week!

Look to the fountain,
Look to the Spring.
There's water for

Swimming,

Fishing,

Drinking,

Washing,

Farming,

Shampooing

and EVERYTHING!

And it's free for the taking,
Unlike before,
When Dee Eel and Sal Mander
Tried to make us all poor.

You see, they were smart,
But we are the wiser;
They thought it a spring,
While we know it's a geyser.

It's been said before that
Avarice makes evil,
So we'll put it more simply:
Greed made them weasels.

But enough already
On the old days of Dry Creek.
From this day forward
Our town is Geyser Creek.

Shout it from mountaintops;
Yodel it in the Great Pyrenees.
We hail from Geyser Creek,
Call us Geyser Creekese!

So that's the story of
Our favorite town.
The ending is happy;
There's no need to frown.

But the tale's not over
Nor our History complete,
Till we tell of a friend
We've been privileged to meet.

Dolcissimo (sweetly)

Her name is Florence,
And she's a friend of our school.
She built our new fountain,
Complete with a pool.

But more important than that
Is the lesson she gives,
Not in the classroom,
But in the way that she lives.

It's a lesson best stated
In words short and plain.
What Flo taught us was this:
The more you give, the more you gain.

Perhaps Ms. Sal Mander
And the slimy Dee Eel
Should ponder those words
The next time they steal.

But wait! Pardon us.
Did we say "next time"?
Oh no, not for those two;
There will be no more crime.

Forte (loudly)

Enter, the Police!
Hark, the siren wail!
We have two new boarders
For the Geyser Creek Jail.

(Enter, the POLICE)

That's it, that's all.
Our story's complete.
Onward to the fountain,
And then, let's all go eat!

IN THE ASSOCIATE CIRCUIT COURT OF ~~DRY~~ *Geyser* CREEK COUNTY, MISSOURI

SEARCH WARRANT

THE STATE OF MISSOURI TO ANY PEACE OFFICER IN THE STATE OF MISSOURI:

WHEREAS, there is probable cause to believe that criminal activity, including:

> Fraud, misrepresentation, greed, and in general, weasel-like conduct and slimy business practices

is being or has been conducted at:

> Dry Creek Water Company and Dry Creek Swimming Pool,

and WHEREAS, the Judge of this Court from the sworn allegations and from supporting written affidavits has found that there is probable cause for the issuance of a search warrant for the purpose of retrieving:

> Written records pertaining to the possible criminal activity

NOW THEREFORE, this search warrant is to command that you search the premises above described within ten days after the issuance of this warrant by day or night, and take with you, if need be, above described property and thereafter return the property so taken and seized by you, together with a duly verified copy of the inventory thereof and with you return this warrant to this Court to be herein dealt with in accordance with the law.

Witness my hand and seal of this Court on the 26th day of May, at 7 p.m.

Judge Anne Chovey

Judge Anne Chovey

RETURN AND INVENTORY

I, *Sting Ray*, being a peace officer within and for ~~Dry~~ *Geyser* Creek County, do hereby return to the above and within warrant as follows: That on the 26th day of May, I went to the premises described therein and searched the same for personal property described therein, and that upon said premises I discovered the following personal property described in the warrant which I then and there took into my possession:

a BAZILLION faxes, letters, memos and miscellaneous correspondence written by Sally Mander and Delbert "Dee" Eel (the rats!)

125

GEYSER
~~DRY~~ CREEK POLICE REPORT

Sheriff Mack Rell

Date: May 26

NAME: Sally Mander
HEIGHT: 5' 5"
WEIGHT: 162 lbs.
FINGERPRINTS:

NAME: Delbert "Dee" Eel
HEIGHT: 6' 2"
WEIGHT: 155 lbs.
FINGERPRINTS:

Mander and Eel booked on charges of fraud, misrepresentation, greed, and in general, weasel-like conduct and
slimy business practices.

Attached: Enlarged photograph (taken and developed
by 5th-grade students) of map in Eel's office
detailing underground water pipes from geyser to
Eel's water company and Mander's pool.

Trial date: Tomorrow.

THE GEYSER CREEK GAZETTE

"We're Gushing With Good News!"
Established Today!

ay 27th Edition   35 Cents

VHAT A DAY! WHAT A FOUNTAIN!

FLORENCE WATERS UNVEILS NEW DRINKING FOUNTAIN
(Photo courtesy of Paddy)

Dry Creek Days opened with a tidal wave urprises.

First was the revelation that Delbert e" Eel and Sally Mander have been con- the citizens of our town (henceforth wn as Geyser Creek) for years.

Using an elaborate underground network ipes, Eel and Mander successfully chan- d water from the recently renamed ser Creek directly to their private busi- es (the water company and swimming , respectively).

he scam, exposed yesterday by a class of graders, deprived residents of Geyser Creek e fresh, clean water that had been theirs for prior to Eel and Mander's construction of Dry Creek Middle School (henceforth n as Geyser Creek Middle School).

he school, built 30 years ago, effective- apped off the geyser at a site directly

beneath a drinking fountain in the main hall-way. The crime was discovered on the occa-sion of replacing the old drinking fountain.

And what a replacement fountain it is! Constructed by Florence Waters, the new drinking fountain is . . . well . . . you have to see it to believe it.

Built around Geyser Creek, the fish-filled fountain is adorned with exotic birds and priceless statues. Visitors to the fountain can swim, fish and even ice-skate on a special temperature-controlled section of the foun-tain. There's a natural whirlpool (look under the weeping willow tree) and a deep end in the fountain, perfect for deep-sea fishing and scuba diving. And in the center of the foun-tain, a geyser (also discovered by the fifth-grade class) spews a column of bubbly water high into the air.

(Continued on page 2, column 1)

(From page 1)

Perhaps most surprising of all is the price of the fountain. When asked how much such an elaborate structure will cost the taxpayers of Geyser Creek, Florence Waters said: "Well, it's free, of course. The students designed it. I just added a few things here and there. Oh, and I brought the walrus, too. His name is Wally. I'm giving him to Mr. Wally Russ. Do you think they'll be friends?"

Upon seeing the fountain and walrus for the first time, eyewitnesses heard Mr. Russ say: "Wha—? Who? How?"

SCENES FROM DRY CREEK DAYS
(Known henceforth as Geyser Creek Days)

SAM'S TUNE-A-COMBO EXPOSES SCAM
(Photo courtesy of Sam N.)

PRINCIPAL WALTER RUSS
MAKES NEW FRIEND
(Photo courtesy of Tad)

Curl and Twirl Reope
Under New Name
Owner Creates Geyse
Inspired Hairsty

PEARL O. STER

Pearl O. Ster heard the news abou geyser just as she was closing the doors beauty shop for the last time.

"At first I thought it was too good true," Ster said. "But then I turned c faucets in my shampoo tubs. They w easy to turn after all these years. But th of a sudden, the glorious water just came bling out! I sat down and washed my hai three times in a row! It's just like th days."

In celebration of the return of free Ster is renaming her hair salon Fountainhead. In addition, Ster is offe special on her original "Geyser-Do."

"It's inspired by the geyser and the tain," said Ster of the hairstyle, which w offered free of charge to anyone who visi Fountainhead this summer.

TO: ~~Dry~~ *Geyser* Creek Inn
Florence Waters
Guest, Room 257

<u>Hand-Delivered</u>

5/27
Good morning, Florence.

I stopped by to see if you'd like to have breakfast with me at the Geyser Creek Cafe, but the hotel clerk told me the kids beat me to it. I'll try to catch up with you (and them) there. There's something I'd like to talk to you about, privately.

In case I miss you at the cafe, remember the Mayor wants to see you and my students in his office at 4:00 this afternoon, after the trial.

Sam

(At the risk of repeating myself, may I tell you once more how spectacular the fountain is? ~~You're~~ It's remarkable.)

GEYSER CREEK MUNICIPAL COURT
Geyser Creek, Missouri

In the case of:

The People of Geyser Creek
versus
Sally Mander and Delbert "Dee" Eel

Honorable Judge Anne Chovey finds both Mander and Eel **GUILTY** on charges of fraud, misrepresentation, greed, and in general, weasel-like conduct and slimy business practices.

Their sentence:

30 years in Geyser Creek County Jail

Special provision:

Mander and Eel will be released under police supervision every afternoon and taken to the Geyser Creek Fountain. There, Mander and Eel will serve snacks and provide towels to fountain visitors. Mander and Eel will also be responsible for picking up any and all debris around the fountain.

OFFICIAL PROCLAMATION

HIS HONOR

MAYOR I. B. NEWT

By the authority vested in me
I hereby bestow the honor and title of

TOWN HISTORIANS

to the
Fifth-Grade Class
of the recently renamed

GEYSER CREEK MIDDLE SCHOOL

Furthermore, I hereby confer the title of

HONORARY CITIZEN OF GEYSER CREEK

to

Florence Waters,
Who so kindly and generously
Donated to our town

THE GEYSER CREEK FOUNTAIN

Which citizens of Geyser Creek
Will enjoy for years to come,
And which will serve as a
Monument to the spirit of giving
And the art of friendship,
Which Florence, Our Friend, has shown to this town.

SIGNED ON THIS DAY,
MAY 27TH

I. B. Newt

_____

Mayor of GEYSER CREEK, MO

'MAY 28 PM

ck # ___cash___

Geyser DRY CREEK FLORIST

DATE: May 28   TIME: 1:20 PM

TO: Florence Waters

ADDRESS: c/o Geyser Creek Inn

FROM: Sam N.

Bouquet of forget - me - nots
+ delivery

8.00
2.00
$ 10.00

Dear Florence,

Hope you'll say yes.

Sam

RETURN T
SENDER

Florence Waters
checked out this morning

132

FIFTH-GRADE ANNOUNCEMENTS

May 31st

LAST DAY OF SCHOOL!

NO HOMEWORK, except daily trips to the Geyser Creek Fountain.*   I'll see you all there.

And NO teasing Mr. Eel or Ms. Mander. (Well, maybe just a little teasing...)

A package has arrived from Florence. We'll open it after we take the History final exam — which I expect all of you to do well on, considering your official status as Town Historians.

> **Mr. N.**

*WORD OF THE DAY: fountain. 1. A spring or source of water. 2. The point of origin of anything.

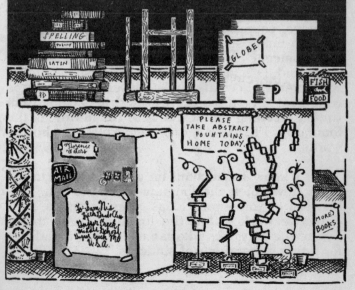

F.W.

To my Fifth-Grade (but First-Class!) Friends:

So sorry I had to leave town in a rush. I wish I could have spent more time with you all, but I've got another fountain to design here in Sri Lanka and not a moment to spare.

First things first: Thank you for a wonderful weekend. I shall never forget my dear friends in Dry Creek – I mean, Geyser Creek.

Now, I have a final favor to ask. It's a big one. As you know, I travel quite a bit. I'm often out of the country for months at a time. That's why I need someone (or someones) to keep an eye on the new Geyser Creek Fountain for me. Would you be willing to do this?

It's a big responsibility. It means, for instance, someone (maybe Lily and Paddy?) will have to make sure the butterflies are well cared for. Someone else (Minnie?) will have to feed the fish. And, Gil, maybe you could be responsible for refilling the chocolate shake dispenser. It's not as complicated as it looks. All the drinks come from the big weeping willow tree near the middle of the fountain. I'll leave a diagram explaining how it works.

I know I can count on your class because I know how much the fountain means to you. It's because of you – your ideas, your drawings, your detective work – that the fountain exists today. You're the only ones who can make sure it endures for future generations of students.

One other thing: In addition to the operating instructions for the fountain, I'm also enclosing pens, pencils and writing paper for everyone. Some of you will want to use these to write more operas. Your first was terrific. (Bravo, Shelly and Tad!) Others may want to write about the past, as you did with "The History of Dry Creek." (Riveting!) How about more investigations? You're all wonderful detectives.

Whatever you do, I hope you'll tell me about it – in words, drawings, photos, or songs. I'll do the same for you, sending you letters and sketches from my travels. That way, we can always be friends no matter how many miles separate us.

Is it a deal? (That's deal, not Dee Eel!) I await your response.

Best regards always,

Florence

P.S. Sam, I'm so pleased you decided to keep your teaching job. You're a wonderful teacher – and a treasured friend. And as for your question: Yes! I'd be delighted to give you painting lessons. I'm sending along a set of watercolor paints for you. Your first assignment is the fountain. Send your masterpiece to me when you finish it.